Dedication

This book is dedicated to my parents, Wayne and Elma Price, who first introduced me to the adventures of family vacations and took me to Mt. Rushmore in 1966. I have since returned four times with various family members who were in awe at this spectacular National Monument.

Thank you to...

My husband, Randy, who still encourages me to live out my dream of introducing children to the national parks, and to my children, Shannon and Bryon, who ate many peanut butter and jelly sandwiches as we traveled thousands of miles to visit "America's Best Idea".

Richard Baldwin, my publisher, and his staff at Buttonwood Press, who prepared this book for printing.

Shannon, Brenda, Gail, and the real Caleb, for their technical support.

Bill and Marcia Pletz for providing camping recipes and tips for outdoor cooking.

The Gumbo Lily book club in Hermosa, SD who read the manuscript and gave it an endorsement.

Rangers at Mt. Rushmore who gave me great information to share.

The children in my life who became the characters in the book.

☆★☆

Chapter 1

Smoke rushed upward, stinging Ben's eyes and causing his lungs to gasp for air. Flames danced higher. The dry wood burned faster than he thought it would, and the blaze was above his head. It was too hot to be near. His campfire was totally out of control.

"Ben, what happened?" yelled his twin sister, Bekka, from fifteen feet away. "Watch out! You're going to get burned!"

Dad was already in motion. "I'll go get a bucket of water."

Mom screamed and came running, a pitcher of lemonade in her hand. With one big wave of her arm, she threw it on the fire. It didn't do much good.

"Mom, why'd you do that? Dad went to get some water."

"I know, but I didn't want it to catch the grass on fire and spread to other campsites."

Just then, Dad arrived with their water bucket ready to douse any sparks that might fly onto the dry grass. Ben looked around to see if anyone else was running over with more buckets.

"I just wanted to have a big enough fire to cook our hot dogs," he sighed.

"Ah, son, with this blaze, I think you could cook enough hot dogs to feed the whole campground." Dad set the bucket down beside the fire pit. "This will have to burn down a while before we can cook anything on it. You stand guard, and be ready to throw water on any sparks that land on the ground. I'm trying to get the camper leveled so our heads aren't tilted downhill when we sleep tonight."

"Okay," Ben replied.

Upon arriving at the campground, everyone had a chore to do before dinner. Dad and Mom opened up the camper and made sure it was level. One time they stopped after dark and couldn't see tree roots above the ground. The camper was not level—one side was higher than the other, making them feel like they could roll off their beds while they were sleeping. From then on, Dad always stopped while it was daylight. Bekka got out folding chairs and set them around the fire pit, while Ben went in search of wood to build a fire. Being a Cub Scout, he put into practice what he had learned on campouts with his pack. Perhaps he had put too much wood on the stack this time, but it seemed like a good idea when he was doing it.

Chapter 2

Ben stared into the fire, his mind swirling with the events of the last two weeks. When school ended for the summer, he thought it was going to be eat, sleep, play, and then get bored. But three days into his vacation, his parents got a call from Uncle Paul, asking Ben and Bekka to meet him at Mount Rushmore on July 2nd. Ben had seen pictures of the heads of presidents carved on Mount Rushmore, and he knew the landmark was famous, but why did his family need to go there?

Ben's uncle was a geologist from South Dakota who traveled around displaying fossil rocks and bones he discovered while digging in the Black Hills. He was really smart and knew about a lot of stuff, so why did he need Ben and Bekka? What was the big deal? And what was the big rush?

For the last two days, while riding in the van from their home in Lansing, Michigan, Ben and Bekka had tried to guess the reason. Their imaginations ran wild. Geologists worked with stones and dirt; maybe Uncle Paul had discovered new dinosaur bones and wanted the twins to see them before they were placed in a museum. Once he had sent them pictures of woolly mammoth skeletons he had dug up—they were huge. Uncle Paul said about a hundred of them were found together in one big area. Maybe he had discovered the biggest one yet.

Gold! Maybe *that* was it! He had heard South Dakota used to be full of gold. Maybe in all of his digging, Uncle Paul had discovered a new gold mine. But why would he want two ten-year-olds there? Definitely not to help him dig. Maybe some gold had come up missing, and Uncle Paul needed two detectives who could help solve the crime. They had some experience at that.

His mother told Uncle Paul how Ben and Bekka had solved the case of the missing band instruments from their school's music room three months before. Drums, flutes, and saxophones had begun disappearing without a clue. The twins figured the caper had to be an inside job, so they waited for the thieves to make a wrong move. Apparently, the night custodian thought no one could see his brother and him as they loaded instruments into a truck after dark. But one night Ben and Bekka watched them through binoculars from Ben's bedroom window across from the school. They called 9-1-1, and the police caught the two thieves red-handed. The instruments were returned just in time for the Spring Concert, making Ben and Bekka heroes. The principal presented each of the twins with a twenty-five dollar savings bond and a Good Citizenship Award. Ben liked being a detective—it had its rewards.

If there's a mystery to be solved, I want to be in on it.

For now though, his job was to build a fire to cook hot dogs for dinner. After driving all day, his parents chose the Twisted Creek Campground in Nebraska to spend the night. Their family enjoyed camping, especially in the summer, when it stayed light so much longer. Nebraska was flat with cornfields growing in every direction. It was way different than Michigan's rolling hills and many lakes.

"Earth to Ben, Earth to Ben," a voice behind him teased, pulling him out of his deep thoughts.

☆☆☆

Chapter 3

Turning, Ben saw his father standing in the doorway of the camper. "I think your fire's ready to cook the hot dogs now. Why don't you test it?"

Always hungry, he didn't need anyone to tell him a second time to get food. He ran to the picnic table where he spotted a package of hot dogs and four long-handled skewers lying together. He ripped open the package, put a hot dog on a skewer, and walked back to his fire.

The flames were still pretty high, but at least they weren't out of control. He put his skewer into the fire about a foot from the ground. The fire near the logs was blue so he knew his hot dog would turn to charcoal if he cooked it down there. He turned the skewer every so often so it would be just the way he liked it. A minute later, he pulled it back out. *Not bad*, he thought, as he inspected it.

"That looks good," his father said, walking toward him with his own hot dog on a skewer, "but how can you see with all this smoke?" Dad waved his arm to clear the air near the fire, then squatted down as low as he could as the smoke circled upward.

"I was doing okay until now. The wind just changed direction. I'm going over to the other side," Ben declared, walking to the opposite side of the fire. He finished cooking his hot dog until it was just the way he liked it.

☆★☆

Ben couldn't wait to start eating. "I'm so hungry, I think I could eat half a pack of hot dogs." He was a growing boy and everything sounded good to eat.

"Ben, I think you're on a 'see-food' diet," Dad said, with a chuckle in his voice. "You see food, and you eat it."

"Very funny," Ben said, standing up and heading for the picnic table, now covered with potato chips, baby carrots, and grapes.

"Hold still, Ben," Bekka said, coming toward him with her new digital camera in hand. She snapped a picture of him looking like the Statue of Liberty holding a hot dog on a stick. "Oh," she sighed, as she looked into the review box on the back of the camera. "Stand still, please, that one was blurry."

"I can't! I'm starving," he complained as she got closer. The smell of the hot dog was killing him. He just had to get a bite, but to keep her happy, he stopped again and smirked.

"Got it!" Looking up at Ben's skewer she remarked, "I'm going to cook my hot dog just like yours."

Bekka was almost like a shadow, wanting to do the same things he did, but then, that was how most twins were. Ben and Bekka looked alike—blond hair and blue eyes—but he was growing taller. Both liked to wear baseball caps—Bekka tucked her ponytail through the strap in the back, and Ben wore his cap to keep the sun out of his eyes. He could hit a ball farther than she could, but she made his glove burn when she threw him pitches.

☆★☆

They did a lot of things together, but schoolwork was something else. He could do multiplication and long division really fast, but she won spelling bees hands-down! He hated spelling tests— he had a brain freeze every Friday, just like clockwork.

Bekka loaded hot dogs onto two skewers. Knowing it wouldn't take long for him to eat his, Ben asked, "Are one of those for me? I'm hungry enough to eat yours *and* mine."

"Not a chance! One's for Mom and one's for me. Mom doesn't like to smell like smoke, but it doesn't bother me," she said, walking toward the fire. She squatted down by her father, who was just about done cooking his hot dog.

Standing up, Dad said, "Hurry with those hot dogs. I think your brother could eat a…"

"NO!" Ben yelled. They turned to see what had happened.

☆★☆

Chapter 4

Ben watched helplessly as a huge brown and black German shepherd dog, standing on his hind legs, ate his long-awaited hot dog from his plate on the table. He had gone into the camper to get the ketchup and mustard, and when he came out, the dog was gobbling down his dinner.

"Get! Go away!" Ben yelled at the dog. "Where did you come from?" he asked, knowing he wouldn't get an answer. The dog looked at Ben, licking the edges of his mouth with a tongue that looked to be a size too long. His tail wagged as if they were friends, and his leash extended down from his collar, beckoning someone to take him for a walk. Ben didn't feel like being his friend—right now *he* wanted to be the one to eat his hot dog!

Dad was by Ben's side in a flash in case the dog was not friendly, but the animal allowed Dad to pull up his collar to check for identification. Mom stepped out of the camper with another pitcher of lemonade in her hand, surprised to see a *guest* for dinner. This meal was proving to be quite eventful.

"So, your name is Buster," Dad said, reading the dog's name tag. "We'll have to walk you over to the office and find your owner before we eat, or all of our hot dogs might go the way Ben's did."

"Good," was all Ben could say as he again loaded up his skewer. This time he took two hot dogs to cook at once. Bekka was done cooking her two and pushed them into buns.

"Trade ya?" Ben asked, hoping she would take him up on his offer. Bekka just snickered.

"I'll take pity on you, Ben," Mom said, offering him hers.

"Thanks," he said, and meant it.

"BUS-TER!" they heard someone yell. Recognizing the voice, Buster jerked against Dad's hold on his leash.

"There you are," a boy said, walking into their campsite area. Dad released the dog and watched it run over to his owner.

"I'm sorry he bothered you." The boy and his dog walked closer to the picnic table. "I was getting him water, and he pulled the stake he was tied to right out of the ground. I've been trying to catch him, but he keeps running away."

"Well, he might not be too hungry now. He just enjoyed Ben's hot dog," Dad said, rubbing the dog's head. Buster nuzzled Dad's leg. "I see his name is Buster. What's yours?"

"Caleb Iron Cloud."

"Nice to meet you, Caleb. It sounds like you are a Native American."

"Yes, I'm a Lakota Sioux Indian," he informed them.

"This is Bekka," Dad said holding his hand over her head. "And this is Ben," doing the same to him. "They're ten years old; how old are you?"

"Nine."

"Looks like Buster has quite a good sniffer. Hold onto him tightly, or you might meet more people at their tables too," Dad said, making everybody laugh. "Maybe we'll see you again before we leave."

"Yeah," Caleb said, heading off with Buster leading the way.

"I wonder where his family is from," Mom said, watching them go.

"I don't know, but can we please eat now?" begged Ben. He thought he might faint from hunger.

☆★☆

Chapter 5

The next morning, Ben and Bekka woke to the smell of bacon cooking. They slept so soundly, they hadn't heard their parents get up. Ben looked out the camper window and saw other families already eating at their tables. Dad and Mom were talking with a jogger while the bacon cooked on the camp stove. It was a perfect summer day with a blue sky and plenty of sunshine.

"Boy, am I hungry," Ben declared, as he crawled out of his sleeping bag. "That bacon smells so good. Come on, Bekka, get up so we can eat."

"Okay," she said sleepily, as Ben bolted out the door. Her sleeping bag felt comfortable, but she knew she'd better hurry if she wanted any bacon. Once Ben sat down to eat, food disappeared. No sooner had these thoughts come to her head than the door opened.

"You'd better hurry," Mom warned Bekka. "There are two hungry men out here ready to wolf down everything in sight." They didn't have to wait long, as Bekka was on her way out of the camper in just a minute.

"Good timing, girl," Dad said, as Ben helped himself to several strips of bacon. "While we eat, let's come up with a plan. Uncle Paul wants to meet us at the Visitor Center at Mt. Rushmore at three o'clock, which means we have to take off in about an hour. Think we can do it?"

★★☆

"Yeah," Ben and Bekka said at the same time. They were anxious to hear all about their mysterious assignment.

In record time the twins rolled up their sleeping bags, while Mom put the food away and Dad packed up the cooking utensils.

"Can we take a walk?" asked Bekka. "We're all ready to go."

"Okay, but you two stay together," cautioned Dad.

"We will," answered Ben, as they set off.

"Look!" Bekka pointed to a sign next to the sidewalk:

'Stay On Sidewalk, Beware of Rattlesnakes.'

"That's kind of scary."

"Aw, they won't bother us if we leave them alone," Ben said, sounding a bit more brave than he really felt. He had no idea what he would do if they heard a snake's tail rattle, other than run. He'd heard stories of people sucking the venom out of snake bites, but that grossed him out. He kept his eyes straight ahead, looking for anything coiled up. As they walked, the burning question of why Uncle Paul wanted to meet them came up.

"Did you think of anything in the night?" Bekka asked.

"Well, it could be he needs two detectives that nobody knows. Maybe something top-secret is happening at Mt. Rushmore. I wish he had given us a clue."

Bekka thought back to what she had read the day before. "The travel book said there are abandoned gold mines around

Mt. Rushmore. Do you think people are hiding in them or stealing gold to get rich?"

"Maybe."

If they solved a mystery, their reporter father could write a story and have it printed in the Lansing newspaper, making them famous. Making headlines in a newspaper sounded cool to Ben. Just then, they realized how far they had followed on the trail and decided to turn back.

"Race you back! Don't let a snake bite ya!" Ben teased, as he took off at a run. Bekka was right on his heels. No snake was going to get her.

Breathlessly, they arrived back at the campsite. Mom and Dad had everything packed up, so the twins helped take down the camper and hitch it to the car.

"It's good to have extra hands to help with this," Dad said, lowering one end of the trailer. "It makes the job go much faster."

Ben and Bekka felt good hearing their help was appreciated. Dad walked around inspecting the latches on each corner, making sure they were securely hooked. He had once told them a story about when he was a boy and his sister hadn't fastened a clip tight enough, causing the top of the camper to fly up while they were traveling. That taught him to check, and sometimes double-check, each latch. The last thing he wanted was to end up on *America's Funniest Videos* with a stranger videotaping their camper looking like an inside-out parachute.

Ben walked around the campsite, making sure they didn't leave anything behind. Being a Cub Scout, he learned you should leave a campsite as clean, if not cleaner, than it was when you arrived. He was sure his pack leader, Mr. Conroy, would ask him about his fires. He was glad they hadn't needed to call the fire department to put out the campfire last night. Bekka would have put that in her journal for sure.

"Looks good to me," Dad proclaimed. "Grab your backpacks from the picnic table. I think we can take off."

Ben and Bekka grabbed their bags and climbed into the van.

"Everybody ready?" Mom asked cheerfully as she slid behind the steering wheel. "Mt. Rushmore, here we come!"

"Wait! Stop!" Ben yelled, opening his window.

Chapter 6

Ben had spied his two new friends heading in the opposite direction. Once again, it looked like Buster was taking Caleb for a walk—not the other way around.

"Caleb! Buster!"

Upon hearing Ben call his name, Buster turned and started running toward their van, with Caleb barely able to hold onto the leash. Buster seemed excited to see Ben again. He put his front paws on the van by Ben's window and tried to lick his face.

"Hi," Caleb said, pulling Buster down. "Are you guys leaving already?"

"Yeah, our uncle wants us to meet him at three o'clock this afternoon, so we have to leave now." Buster jumped up one more time, and Ben rubbed his head.

Dad turned his head toward Ben. "Wish we had time to talk, but we gotta go."

"Bye," both boys said at the same time, and then shortly the Coopers' van and trailer left Twisted Creek Campground behind.

"I like Buster and Caleb," Ben said sadly. "I wish we could've stayed here longer. Can we get a dog like Buster?"

"We'll have to think seriously about that," Mom said, looking in the rearview mirror at Ben. "If we got a dog, it would have to be small enough so it couldn't eat food off the table by standing on its hind legs."

"Yeah," piped up Bekka. "Remember when Hannah's dog ate her birthday cake? Her mom screamed like crazy and had to go buy one for the party." Their friend's dog, which looked like a small horse, had eaten half of the birthday cake from the counter when Hannah's mother wasn't looking. That was a birthday to remember.

"I'd train it to leave people food alone," Ben promised, hoping to impress his parents. Caleb was lucky to have a dog, even if he was a hot dog thief.

Bekka wasted no time getting out her travel book and journal. She liked to write down names of the state license plates they saw on cars. She saw fifteen different ones the first day of their trip, and yesterday, she added seven more—New York, Ohio, Iowa, Utah, Texas, Florida, and Mississippi. She had fun writing that last one. She learned to spell it by saying M-i-double-s-i-double-s-i-double-p-i. That's how a spelling bee champion did it!

Ben was happy with his video games—the more action, the better. His mother suggested it might be good for him to journal things to remember about this trip, but so far, nothing exciting had happened. Maybe Buster eating his hot dog would be funny to remember. If his teacher assigned him to write an essay on his vacation, he would write five easy words, *"A dog ate my dog."* He smiled at his cleverness. He was almost at the end of a video game when Bekka interrupted his thoughts.

She had been reading about South Dakota in her travel book and came upon something interesting to tell them. She called it FYI—*For Your Information.*

"This is a quiz. What does the 'Mt.' stand for in Mount Rushmore?" Before she gave anyone a chance to respond, in her excitement, she gave away the answer, "Mount! Mt. is short for Mount, as in Mount Rushmore, get it?"

"Got it," Ben grunted.

Continuing her quiz, she asked, "Whose faces are on Mt. Rushmore?"

"Washington," Ben blurted out before his parents could answer. He remembered that one from a calendar. He'd let his parents add the others, since he didn't know them.

"Lincoln," Mom added.

"Jefferson, I think," Dad answered, but no one could think of the other president.

"Give up?" Bekka asked, sounding like a *Miss Know-It-All*. "It's President Roosevelt, but do you know which one since there were two presidents named Roosevelt?"

"Oh yeah, it's Theodore, but everyone called him Teddy," Dad answered. "And do you know what is special about him compared to the others?"

"Yes," Bekka answered.

"That's because you're looking at a picture," Ben responded. He had no idea what Teddy Roosevelt looked like. "Does he have a huge wart on his nose?"

"No," his sister answered back as she showed Ben the book. "He has on glasses. Look, they're huge."

Out of curiosity, Ben looked at President Roosevelt's glasses. How could they look so real being carved in stone?

Bekka took the book back. "Okay, do any of you know why they were chosen to be on the mountain?"

No one answered because they weren't sure.

"FYI—President Washington was chosen because he was the first president. President Lincoln was president during the Civil War and preserved our country from becoming two nations. President Jefferson wrote the Declaration of Independence and believed in the expansion of our country. And Teddy Roosevelt is there because he believed in the development of our country."

"This is too much like school," Ben complained. His brain was on vacation!

"One last FYI: how tall are the faces of the presidents?"

"150 feet," guessed Ben.

"Seriously?" Bekka shot back at him. Ben raised his eyebrows at her and smirked.

"I'd say 50 feet," guessed Mom.

"Close—they're 60 feet," Bekka informed them.

"That's taller than our house," Dad calculated. "In fact, it's three times as tall as our house. One thing for sure, I'm glad I didn't have to work on it."

"Yeah," Bekka remarked, as she looked at a picture of a man with a rope tied around his waist hanging off President Lincoln's nose. It looked like he was bobbing around. *Spiderman would have had a great time out there.* She giggled as she imagined the web he could sling around Abe's face.

Looking up from his game, Ben called out as they passed a large sign, "Yay, we're in South Dakota! I thought we'd never get here. How much farther, Mom?"

"About sixty miles. Anybody hungry for lunch? I just saw a sign for burgers, tacos, and subs. What sounds good?"

"Tacos," Bekka said. Soft-shell tacos were the best!

"Burgers," Ben said with gusto. He wanted one with every-thing on it.

"A sub," Dad said, casting a vote for his favorite sandwich.

"Good," Mom said, turning into a travel center that advertised all three. "This place has everything we want."

The Coopers stood in line and ordered their favorite foods. No one was disappointed with their choices, and they ate like they hadn't seen food for days.

"We should live here," Ben said, daydreaming about the meals he could get each day.

"I wouldn't want to. There isn't any ice cream," Bekka retorted. She was addicted to chocolate ice cream and had to have some almost every day. Maybe she could talk Mom into stopping at a Dairy Queen for a Blizzard. They tasted so good on a hot summer day. While crossing Nebraska, she imagined pioneer families traveling dusty trails in covered wagons, and how women and girls wore long dresses and bonnets. It made her hot just thinking about it.

Stepping back out into the eighty-five-degree temperatures, everyone was glad their van had air-conditioning. Ben and Bekka raced back to their vehicle, but dropped their jaws and stared when they got near it. Dad and Mom were equally surprised. No one could believe their eyes.

☆★☆

Chapter 7

"A flat tire," Mom exclaimed, looking at her watch. "We don't have *time* for a flat tire!" Though they didn't have many miles to go, they were about to enter the Black Hills with its twisting and winding roads, and no one dared go fast with cliffs on the other side of the guardrails.

"All right, let's work together and get it changed in record time," Dad declared. "If we have trouble, we're here at a service center and can get help."

"But it's *hot*," Bekka said, not wanting to be too whiny, even though she felt that way.

"I know, but let's get going." Dad got out the tools to remove the tire from under the van. Ben tried to loosen the lug nuts on the flat tire, but it was harder than it looked when someone did it on TV. Bekka held the new tire by the back of the car while Dad took over for Ben and removed the flat one, then put on the replacement. Mom went into the travel center to get everyone a cold bottle of water. Within a half-hour, they were back on the road.

"I'll drive while you sightsee," Dad told Mom, who pulled her camera out of her bag since she liked to take pictures of scenery.

Ben went back to his video game, while Bekka looked out the window at road signs which were everywhere, advertising anything that visiting tourists might want to see.

"Hey, I just saw a sign about gold. Do you think we'll find gold lying around?"

"It's doubtful, but you never know," Dad replied. "Does your book say when gold was discovered here?" He liked to know some of the history of places their family visited, so he was pleased Bekka had her travel book handy.

Finding a chapter about South Dakota gold, Bekka read, "'Gold was first discovered in 1874 by an army scout traveling with General George Custer. He bent over to get a drink from the French Creek in the Black Hills and saw something shiny. It was gold!'" *Boy! Was he lucky,* she thought.

"Mom, what's Black Hills gold jewelry?" Bekka asked, after reading a billboard advertising it.

"It's jewelry made from a special mixture of gold, silver, and copper, I think it is, to make green-and-peach-colored leaves beside clumps of grapes—a design they put on rings, necklaces, and watches. They've been doing it for many years. Grandma had a ring made from Black Hills gold and I thought I might get one while we're here."

"I heard there are old mines where you can pan for gold. Want to try your hand at that?" asked Dad.

"How do you do it?" Ben asked, looking out the windows at hills he hoped were full of gold.

"At a gold mine, buckets of dirt are dug out of the mine. A scoop of dirt is put into a shallow pan, like a frying pan without a handle. Water is poured into it, and you swish it around and around, tipping the pan slightly so the water and dirt come out little by little. Gold is heavier than dirt, so it settles to the bottom. If you see anything shiny, it's gold, and you get to keep it. That's panning for gold. Sounds like fun. Want to try it?"

"Yeah!" Ben exclaimed. "Wouldn't it be cool if we found a really big hunk of gold? We'd be rich." Just thinking about it made him excited. New video games, a new bike, a fancy skateboard, and a faster scooter. Panning for gold was now on his list of things to do!

"This book says the first nuggets were the size of pine cones." Bekka's eyes got really big thinking about that possibility. "I bet we'd be millionaires."

"That would make the front page of the newspaper for sure," Mom said, noticing the landscape was changing. It wasn't flat any longer, and she could see dark mountains in the distance. "What does your book say about the Black Hills? These aren't just hills; they look like mountains to me."

Bekka was getting to be a pro at looking up facts in her travel book. Looking out the window to see what she had just read she said, "For everyone's information, these are Ponderosa pine trees. Some are 800 years old and ten feet across. The tallest ones are 134 feet high."

"Impressive, most impressive," Dad said, quoting one of his favorite movie lines.

☆☆☆

Passing an Indian tepee and trading post, Mom asked, "What kind of Indians live here?"

"This used to be sacred burial grounds for the Lakota Indians. Colonel George Custer led an expedition here in 1874. He made peace treaties with the Indians, but they were later broken when gold was discovered. Everybody wanted to get rich quick!"

Dad pulled the van to a stop to pay an entrance fee. "Speaking of Colonel Custer, we are about to enter Custer State Park." Hoping to see the animals the park was famous for, he followed the sign to Wildlife Loop. After driving a few miles, he said, "Something is missing." He looked around and continued, "What's brown with horns and has hundreds of legs?"

Ben looked up from his game and looked around to see what his father was talking about. All he saw were tall trees and fallen rocks by the road.

"Here's a second clue—think silver, it makes sense." Dad thought he was so clever, knowing one word could be spelled two ways. Bekka and Ben looked at each other, thinking they knew the answer.

"Third clue—your mom would rather buy a Black Hills gold ring than cuddle up with one of these," Dad said.

Guessing the answer, Ben spoke up, "I'd rather see a buffalo than a fancy ring. Do you think we'll see any?"

"We might. I've heard there are herds of them here in Custer State Park," answered Dad. "In case you didn't see the sign, we're on Wildlife Loop. We'll have to keep our eyes open as we drive through the mountains. I saw a sign advertising buffalo burgers. Want to try one?"

"Buffalo burgers, ee-ew," squealed Bekka. "No thank you."

"Me either," agreed Ben.

"Do you think it tastes like a regular burger?" Mom asked. She turned and grimaced at Ben and Bekka.

"I don't know. If we find a restaurant that serves them, I'll order one and you three can share it with me," remarked Dad. "We'll pretend we're a pioneer family living out on the prairie, and buffalo is the only meat we have to eat. Ben, you can have the first bite, okay?" He loved to tease Ben about eating.

"No way," he exclaimed. "I'd rather see one than eat one!"

"Me too," agreed his sister. They had a feeling buffalo burgers would probably taste funny.

Just then, Bekka's upper body jerked across the seat. Dad turned sharply to miss a huge boulder that had fallen from a mountain. If she hadn't had her seatbelt on, her nose would have been plastered up against the side window, just like Garfield.

"Dad!" Bekka screamed, as they turned around another very sharp curve.

☆★☆

Chapter 8

Dad slammed on the brakes and stopped the van. A herd of buffalo was crossing the road. They couldn't believe what was happening. One by one, the buffalo walked right in front of their van.

"Co-ol!" exclaimed Ben, as he unbuckled his seatbelt to get a better view of animals that once roamed the Great Plains in large herds. He couldn't believe he was so close to a real live buffalo.

"They're huge! Look how big their horns are!" His eyes were almost bulging out of his head.

"Where's my camera?" Bekka frantically searched her backpack. Dad put down the side window so she could get a better view when she was ready to take a picture.

Mom grabbed for her camera and got a few pictures from the windshield. One buffalo came within two feet of the front of the van.

"I can't believe this," Ben exclaimed, watching them walk by. "How much do you think they weigh?"

"I've heard bulls weigh more than a thousand pounds. Imagine if one charged at our van."

"I'd freak out."

"Look at the baby ones," Bekka squealed while watching two small calves follow close behind their mothers. "Wow, perfect timing," she said as three huge bulls turned and looked at her as she raised her camera. They were so close all she got was heads and horns. She was amazed this was happening. The buffalo weren't in a hurry. They didn't care that they had stopped traffic and a huge line of cars formed behind the Coopers' van.

"Wait 'til I tell my friends. They won't believe me!" Ben said, watching the last of the herd meander out of sight. "I'll have to show them pictures to prove we were this close to them." For once, all the pictures his mother and sister took would come in handy.

☆☆☆

Mom set her camera in the cup holder next to her seat. "One should be armed and ready to shoot a picture of wildlife when it crosses your path. I'm leaving my camera right beside me in case we see an elk or something else with long horns. Getting that close to buffalo was awesome."

"Yep," Dad said, as he drove cautiously forward. "They were brown, had horns, hundreds of legs, and you wouldn't want to cuddle up with one. I'll give a nickel to the first one who can figure out what the second clue, 'it's silver and makes sense' means."

Ben and Bekka had to think about that one. Mom opened her purse and looked through her coins. She gave each of them a nickel. Bekka came up with the answer first. "I get it. It's silver and has a buffalo on it. And a nickel is five cents."

"Bingo—you get to keep your nickel."

Ben groaned. *Where did his father get these ideas?*

"If I had to give clues about another animal, I'd say, 'when you eat, you do this to your food, Ben.' You wolf it down."

"Funny, very funny," Ben said, rolling his eyes.

The hills were getting steeper, and the turns were very sharp. Bekka tried to look over the edge of the road, but they were so high up into the mountains, it scared her.

Without warning, Mom called out, "Stop the van."

⭐⭐☆

Chapter 9

Ben jerked his head to see what was in front of them now. "What are we doing?"

"Let's get a picture at the Mt. Rushmore National Monument sign," Mom suggested. Dad pulled the van to a stop. "I think we'll do this each time we go to a National Park and start a collection of pictures."

Ben groaned, but Bekka grabbed her camera, thinking it was a sensational idea.

"It'll be a fun picture to have in our photo album," Mom remarked. "Maybe we'll put it in our Christmas cards."

Ben groaned again. He just knew his grandmas would call and tell him how cute he was and say, *"My how you've grown."*

They piled out of the van and waited as another father took his family's picture.

"Would you like to get in the picture with your family?" Dad asked the other father.

"Thanks, that would be great. I'll do the same for you."

"Ready?" Dad asked the other family as they surrounded the sign. "Everybody say, 'cheese'." A chorus of *cheese* came through cheesy smiles. Dad and Bekka gave the man their cameras. Ben jumped up on top of the sign and Bekka climbed up next to him. It was wide enough for their feet to stand securely. Dad and Mom just stood on the ground and smiled.

"Thanks, guys," Mom said as she fastened her seatbelt. "It's a mom-thing to want a family photo."

Dad looked into the rearview mirror and pulled out onto the road. "From here on, this is a nonstop ride to the top. Mt. Rushmore, here we come."

Climbing higher into the Black Hills, and passing signs directing them to Mt. Rushmore, Bekka tried to guess which one would have the faces of the presidents on the other side.

"I think I see Mt. Rushmore," exclaimed Ben excitedly looking through his binoculars in an open area.

"Let me see, let me see," begged Bekka.

"Look right over there," he pointed as he handed them to her.

"Wow! It really is Mt. Rushmore." She could make out the four faces way in the distance. After traveling for two-and-a-half days, they were almost there. She could hardly wait. She decided right then and there, she needed a picture of herself by Mt. Rushmore. She was going to begin a new collection—pictures of herself in famous places. She'd hang them up and call it her Wall of Fame. Nobody she knew had a Wall of Fame. She'd be the first.

"Bekka, we're here. Let's go," Ben said, opening his door. Grabbing her camera, she hopped out of the car.

Chapter 10

"It's huge," Bekka gasped, truly amazed at just how big Mt. Rushmore was.

"Yeah," Ben agreed. It was nothing like looking at it in a picture. "How could anybody get way up there and carve those faces in a stone mountain? That must be a mile high." They felt like ants.

Along with a lot of other visitors, they followed signs to the Visitor Center. Flags from the fifty states lined the Avenue of Flags walkway. They felt like they were in a parade. Bekka decided she and Ben needed to get a picture by the Michigan flag.

People passed them eating ice cream cones.

"Can we please have some ice cream?" Bekka begged, with her hands folded under her chin. It was *so hot,* and those ice cream cones looked *so good.*

"We'll get some on our way back to the van," Dad replied. "With it being this warm, the ice cream would melt and run down your arm. Besides, we're supposed to be in the Visitor Center right now. It's three o'clock—we made it just on time." Keeping the deadline with Uncle Paul was important. Ben and Bekka couldn't wait—in only a few more minutes, the mystery of why they were to meet him would be revealed.

Stepping inside the building, Ben spread his arms out from his sides, enjoying the cool air-conditioned building. "Ah-h, this feels so good. I might stay in here all day."

"I'm with you," Mom agreed.

They began looking for Uncle Paul. Not seeing him right away, they stopped to look at exhibits describing how workers dynamited and carved the faces in the mountain.

Just then, a park ranger, dressed in his uniform and hat, walked through with a crowd of kids. They could hear him talking about Mt. Rushmore and pointing out the window at it.

"I wonder what they're doing?" Ben asked.

"I don't know, I'll ask at the information desk." Mom said, heading in that direction.

The ranger behind the counter told her it was part of the Junior Ranger program for boys and girls ages five to twelve. He pulled out a couple of booklets and turned to Ben and Bekka who had come over to stand by her.

"National parks are taken care of by trained rangers who enlist the help of young people to help protect wildlife and keep the park clean and safe for other visitors. It's called the Junior Ranger program. You attend a ranger-led activity and watch a film about Mt. Rushmore. As you walk around the park, you work on the things in this booklet. It has projects to do, things to find, animals to identify, and other activities to try while you're here. When you're done, bring it back to the desk, and you'll receive a certificate and can buy a Junior Ranger patch."

"Cool," Ben said, half listening, half looking at the booklet.

The ranger continued, "There are some important rules to remember about a national park: no one is to remove anything from the park; you can't pick wildflowers or plants; stay on trails to protect the plants that are growing; and, as Junior Rangers, be our eyes and ears if you see anything suspicious."

☆★☆

"Hey, I want to do that," Bekka said flipping her booklet open.

"Me too," Ben said. "Can Junior Rangers climb to the top of the mountain?"

"I don't think that's part of the program," said Mom, relieved to know they wouldn't need a helicopter rescue of her son off Roosevelt's glasses.

"Wow, this has fun things to do," said Bekka excitedly, looking at a clever game to play. "Let's get started on it while we wait for Uncle Paul to get here."

"Yeah," agreed Ben. He turned and saw the presidents looking at him through the window which went from the floor to the high ceiling. Just then, a hand clamped down upon his shoulder. A chill went shivering up his spine. He whirled, ready to defend himself.

✩★✩

Chapter 11

"Uncle Paul!" he exclaimed, relieved to see a familiar face. "You made it."

"Sorry I'm late," he apologized, giving Ben's shoulders a hug. "I was held up working on a project in Deadwood. I spotted you in the window and thought I'd surprise you."

"You freaked me out!"

"Paul!" Mom rushed over to hug her brother while Dad shook his hand.

"It's good to see you, Amy and Dan. I'm glad you all could make it."

Seeing Bekka standing next to her mother, he grabbed her in a hug, too. "How's my favorite niece doing?"

"Good," was all she could get out before he pulled her and Ben together to inspect how tall they had grown. *Why do grown-ups always do that?*

"You're going to be as tall as I am if you keep growing like this," he joked. Both knew it would be a long time before that happened, so they just smiled.

Uncle Paul was a bit taller than their dad and had a great big grin. He was tanned and wore a big cowboy hat. He looked like he had just come from a rodeo.

"I hope you had a good trip. Where are you guys staying?" he asked.

"In Keystone," Dad answered. "We have reservations at the Circle M Campground."

"That's good. It's not too far from here. I have a room at a hotel in town, so we'll be close to each other. I might even join you out at a campfire one evening. Did you see any wildlife on your way up here?"

"You wouldn't *believe* all the buffalo we saw," Bekka blurted out excitedly.

"Yeah, we were just driving on a road and all of a sudden, there was a whole herd of them crossing the road," cut in Ben, his voice getting excited remembering what they saw. "We had to slam on the brakes so we didn't hit them! It was awesome."

"Wow. It's great you saw them. Some people spend a week here and never see even one," he assured them. "So, what have you seen around Mt. Rushmore?"

"Nothing. We just arrived a half-hour ago," explained Mom.

"That's good, because I want to be your personal guide," he said with enthusiasm. "I work near Mt. Rushmore each summer and I know the best places to visit. Before we get started, Ben and Bekka, you might want to check out the Junior Ranger program. It's something kids like to do, and you'll learn a lot about the park."

☆★☆

"We already signed up," Bekka said, excited to show him her booklet.

"Great. Now, how many days are you staying around here?" he asked as he looked through it.

"At least three days," answered Dad. "We want to stay until the Fourth of July to see the fireworks. I have heard they are spectacular over Mt. Rushmore."

"If you wait to see the fireworks on the Fourth of July here at Mt. Rushmore, you won't see any, because they set them off on the *third* of July. That way, they don't do it at the same time the towns around here set off *their* fireworks," Uncle Paul explained.

Ben's curiosity couldn't wait any longer. "So, why did you want us to come here?" he asked, looking up into his tall uncle's face. Ben's head was tipped way back, his hands were on his hips, and his eyebrows were scrunched together.

"The answer to that question will have to wait until tomorrow."

"What?" the twins said together. Their voices were just a bit too loud, making heads turn toward them. That wasn't what they wanted to hear.

"But we want to know now," begged Ben. "You're *killing* us. We can't *wait* until tomorrow."

"Yeah," Bekka added. "Why do we have to wait 'til tomorrow?"

"You'll just have to wait and see." He smiled with a twinkle in his eye, looking at their parents. Changing the subject, he said,

"Since we're here, let's find a ranger and begin working on your assignments."

Uncle Paul turned to find one. He was tall enough to see over the heads of most of the people in the room.

Spotting a ranger first, Ben said, "Hey, there's one over by the drinking fountain," and headed off to ask when they could get started.

"Hey, I'm coming too," Bekka said, taking off to catch up with him.

☆★☆

Chapter 12

The ranger spotted Ben and Bekka coming toward him with their booklets in hand. "What's this, two eager Junior Rangers?" he asked, smiling at them.

"Yes," the twins said together.

"Hi, I'm Ranger Phil, and I'll be your tour guide this afternoon. What are your names?"

"Bekka."

"Ben."

"It's good to have you with us at Mt. Rushmore. Where are you from?"

"Lansing, Michigan," Ben answered,

"Really? I have a sister who lives in Lansing, and she has two children near your ages, Shannon and Bryon. They came here once just to watch the fireworks. They thought they were awesome. Are you coming back to see the fireworks tomorrow night? I hope so. You've never seen anything like it."

"Yeah, I guess we are," Bekka answered, looking at Ben. At least she was pretty sure they were, now that Uncle Paul had talked about them.

"Good. Okay, let's get started. It's a great day to be here—blue sky and sunny. Three days ago, it was so foggy you couldn't see the faces at all. Everybody was bummed. Some families had driven a thousand miles and could only see up to those trees over there. Keep your binoculars handy. The guide will point out things, but you can see them a whole lot better with binoculars."

Ben gave the ranger a big toothy grin, glad he had remembered to bring theirs. Eager to use them, he asked, "When can we start?"

"Well, so you know what it took to carve Mt. Rushmore, we suggest you watch the video about its construction. It began in 1927, long before there were cranes and machines like we have today. That mountain is made of granite. It took lots of dynamite to blast away what wasn't needed. The video will begin in ten minutes in the theater. I think you'll find it to be very interesting."

"Okay," Mom said, looking at her watch.

"While you're waiting, why don't you step in here and look at the exhibits," Ranger Phil said, directing them to a room filled with pictures and tools used in the construction.

Looking at Ben and Bekka he asked, "Do you have any idea how Mt. Rushmore got its name?" They looked at each other and shrugged their shoulders.

"Mr. Charles Rushmore, a lawyer from New York, was here in the Black Hills on an assignment and he met the sculptor.

The sculptor liked Mr. Rushmore, so he named it after him. How would you like to have a monument named after you?"

"That'd be sweet," Bekka said, thinking of her Wall of Fame.

"Do either of you know how many men worked on creating Mt. Rushmore?"

"Four hundred," burst out Bekka.

"You got that right, but do you know how many died?"

"None," she answered with a smile. She knew she was right.

"Boy, you're good," congratulated the ranger.

"She read it in her book," Ben commented, wishing he had known at least one of the answers.

Turning to Ben, Ranger Phil asked, "Do you know who the sculptor was?"

"Not exactly, but I know it's a funny name." Bekka had told him what it was in one of her FYI moments, but it didn't stick in his brain.

"You're right, it is unusual, but I won't tell you since it's the answer to a question in your Junior Ranger book. You'll learn more about it at the Sculptor's Studio. Now, I have to go see about getting the movie started." With that, he walked through a door and closed it behind him.

Looking at a picture of some men climbing a rope ladder up the outside of Abraham Lincoln's head, Ben said to his uncle,

"Wow, that's so cool! I wish I could take a rope and go out there like that."

"Do you think you'd be afraid?" Uncle Paul asked.

"Not me. That looks like fun—bouncing around on his nose."

Bekka wasn't so sure about being out there. "What if those ropes broke? How'd they get back up? I bet they wished they had cranes back then. It would have been a lot easier."

"You're right," her uncle said. "Just imagine what it took to chisel those noses and put glasses on Roosevelt. I bet some of those men were scared the first time they were lowered down over the edge."

"Yeah," Bekka said, thinking about how far down it was from up there.

"I wouldn't have been scared," answered Ben. "I think it would be cool to climb all the way to the top. Do you think you could do it, Uncle Paul?"

After a moment, he replied, "Being a geologist, I've done my share of climbing and looking at rocks, but I don't think I'd like to climb Mt. Rushmore. It's hundreds of feet up to the top, and that's slippery granite. I prefer to keep my feet on the ground, thank you. Besides, it's against the law to climb it."

"Rats," Ben said, disappointed he couldn't climb it. He was convinced he could do it if they'd let him.

"Look into President Lincoln's eyes," Uncle Paul said. "See anything?"

"No," Ben and Bekka answered together, stepping closer to the picture to see if anything showed up.

"I didn't think so," he answered, smiling at them. "The sculptor had a great idea to build a secret vault inside the mountain behind the heads. He wanted to hide special documents like the United States Constitution, the Bill of Rights, and the Declaration of Independence in it."

"Really? He really put a secret hiding place in there?" asked Bekka. She had never heard about a secret vault in Mt. Rushmore.

"He sure did."

"Why?" asked Ben.

"He thought it would be a good idea to have copies in there in case the real ones were destroyed."

"Are they still there now?" Bekka asked again.

"Yes. To tell you the truth, the sculptor began carving the vault, but ran out of money and died soon after. His son finished Mt. Rushmore and years later they finished the secret vault, calling it the Hall of Records. Movies have been made here at Mt. Rushmore and some people wanted to go into the vault, but they couldn't because it's a protected place. You might want to write a report on it for school sometime. Your teacher would be amazed you even know about it."

As Uncle Paul talked, Ben and Bekka stared at Mt. Rushmore. *Who knew all this?* Listening to her uncle, Bekka was convinced he was probably the smartest man she knew. Other than her dad, of course.

"The video is about to begin," Mom said, coming toward them.

Everyone went into the theater and chose their seats. It was amazing to watch how a stone mountain was carved into a monument with faces that looked like real people.

"If they had movies like this at school, I totally wouldn't mind learning about history and geography," whispered Ben to Bekka. She agreed.

As the narrator continued, Ben pictured himself up there on a rope, setting off dynamite and chiseling away at Washington's nose. *What if someone chipped it off by accident?* He almost laughed out loud thinking about "no-nose" George.

☆★☆

Chapter 13

When the lights came on, Bekka and Ben were anxious to go outdoors and get started on a hike. Ten other Junior Rangers stood by Ranger Phil who began giving directions and led them and their parents outside to the trail below Mt. Rushmore. His first caution was for everyone to stay on the paved trails and not walk on the grass. He explained that rangers work hard to keep the prairie grasses and wildflowers growing in their natural surroundings. He instructed them not to litter and they were definitely not to set a fire anywhere in the park. Fire danger is always higher in the summer.

"Ben, do you have the binoculars?" Mom asked, as they followed the ranger.

"No, I left them in the theater," he groaned, surprised he had forgotten them. "I'll go get them." Running back into the building, he hoped they were still there. He was in luck because, when he got there, the lights were on and only a couple guys were seated, waiting for the video to start again. He had put the binoculars on the floor under his seat, so he searched for the row where his family had sat. While he looked, he couldn't help overhearing the men talking. They spoke softly, but it sounded like they were coming up with a diabolical plan.

"We'll start when the fireworks start," he heard one man say.

"You sure no one will hear us?" asked the other man.

"How can they? Fireworks are so loud, no one can tell the difference between them and dynamite."

"We'll be rich."

What were they planning to do? Ben wondered as he bent low to look under the seats. *Were they terrorists planning to blow up Mt. Rushmore or blast into the Hall of Records? Should he report what he heard or just keep it to himself?* He wanted to stay longer and listen, but knew it would look suspicious.

"Hey kid, lose something?" one of the men called out to him.

"Ah-h, no, I found it," he stammered, as he reached for the binocular case. He wished he didn't have to walk past them, but it was the only way out of the theater. He took a deep breath as he stood up. *Don't let them know you heard anything,* he told himself and hurried up the aisle. As he got near their row, he looked at them and then turned away. He got a good look at one of them, but not the other. Passing under the exit sign, he let out a sigh of relief—he was glad to get out of there. Those guys gave him the creeps.

Spotting his family down the trail, he hurried to catch up with them. He tried to act like nothing had happened, but his sister knew him too well.

"You look like you saw a ghost. What happened?"

"I heard two guys talking about blowing up something during the fireworks."

"Are you sure?"

"Yeah, they were talking about the fireworks covering up the noise."

"What noise?"

"I don't know. They said something about dynamite, then saw me and quit talking."

Ben looked behind them to make sure they weren't being overheard or followed. Not seeing anyone that looked like the man in the theater, he relaxed and listened to the guide talk about the many years it took to blast through the mountain and to carve the four faces.

Mom used the binoculars to get a better look at Washington's nose and Roosevelt's glasses as the guide described them. Ben and Bekka walked on ahead and waited to begin climbing the steps toward the Sculptor's Studio. The guide explained there were two hundred steps up to the Studio and almost another two hundred back to the Visitor Center. He advised that only those in good shape should try it.

"Hey, you two, stop! I want to get your picture." The twins twirled around as their uncle raised his camera. "Smile, you look good with the four presidents behind you."

"Can you take some with my camera?" Bekka asked. "I want a picture of the two of us and then one of just me."

☆★☆

Uncle Paul had to wait as other visitors passed by. He took the picture of the twins just as a man walked behind them, so he took another.

When he took her shot alone, Bekka did one of her famous "ta-dah" poses. The title "President Bekka Cooper" flashed through her mind, and she smiled.

"Do you guys think you can handle four hundred steps?" Mom asked.

"Sure," answered Bekka, as she began climbing them.

"Me, too," Ben said, as he shot past her.

"Aren't you hungry?" asked Dad. "I'm starving." The twins were well on their way to the Sculptor's Studio, so their parents had no choice but to follow.

"I think I'm going to call it quits for now," remarked Uncle Paul. "I'll meet you at my hotel before dinner."

"Sounds good to me," Dad answered, taking off after the twins, but then stopping to wait for Mom.

"Oh," she said taking a hold of Uncle Paul's arm. "What hotel are you staying at?"

"Oh yeah, it would be helpful if you knew where I'm staying," he laughed. "It's the Soaring Eagle in Keystone, Room 225. I'll see you in about an hour." He looked at his watch before turning back toward the trail leading to the parking lot.

"We're going to have to step it along to catch the twins," Dad called over his shoulder as he began heading up the steps. "Only three hundred and ninety more steps 'til we're back to the Visitor Center. Why do ten-year-olds have so much more energy than their parents?"

☆★☆

Chapter 14

Ben and Bekka were looking around the Sculptor's Studio when their parents walked in. Ben wrote *Gutzon Borglum* in the space for the answer to the sculptor's name in his Junior Ranger book. "No wonder I couldn't remember his name. Why didn't his mother name him something easy, like *Ben*?"

"That would be easier to spell," Bekka agreed.

Mom looked at the models of the four presidents' heads, which were made back in the 1920s. She couldn't believe they were still in such good shape.

"That's a lot of Play-Doh," Ben remarked, taking note that the clay models were taller than he was. And they looked just like the faces out on the monument.

"The more I learn about Mt. Rushmore and what it took to create it, the more amazed I am at the project," Mom concluded.

"You might be amazed, but I'm hungry," remarked Dad, coming up behind her and the twins. "It's been a long time since lunch, and those steps are a killer. We're supposed to meet Uncle Paul at his hotel in less than an hour. We'll come back tomorrow. The ranger said there's another trail we might want to take."

"Okay," Bekka said, looking for the name of a certain kind of jackhammer to write her last answer in the book. She went over to a display case and looked for a name tag.

⭐⭐⭐

Once again, the mention of food got a quick response from Ben. He closed his book and was ready to leave in an instant.

"We're going to need to stop at a hardware store on the way to the campground," Mom said on the way to the parking lot. "Our flashlight batteries are getting weak. I want new ones, since it gets pretty dark out here. I hope coyotes don't come into the campground. They sound cool when they howl, but I just don't want to see one slinking around our camper."

"Me, either," Bekka agreed. Seeing several people walk by with ice cream cones, her craving returned. Turning to her father she said, "Ice cream, remember your promise?"

"But what about your appetite for dinner?" Mom teased.

"It won't ruin mine," Ben said. Nothing spoiled his appetite.

"You're right, a promise is a promise," Dad said. "What flavor do you want?"

"Chocolate," the twins said in unison.

"Okay, two chocolates and two vanillas it is." He knew Mom's favorite, too.

It didn't take long to get their ice cream, and soon they were headed toward Keystone.

Ben and Bekka looked at Mt. Rushmore for as long as it was in view, and then turned their attention to video games as their father zigzagged his way down the mountain roads. Ten minutes later they were at a hardware store in Keystone.

☆★☆

As their parents looked for batteries, the twins wandered around. Bekka stopped to smell candles while Ben went in search of his favorite candy bar. Rounding a corner, he stopped dead in his tracks as he spotted the man from the theater at the other end of the aisle. He quickly looked away, but Ben knew it was him. The man had an unforgettable face: dark eyes, big eyebrows, and a pointy nose. The stranger noticed Ben's quick movement. They made eye contact for a split second, but that was long enough. Ben wondered if the guy recognized him.

Ben retraced his steps toward his sister. Her eyes widened when she saw his face. "What happened to you? You see another ghost?"

"It's him—he's here. Here in the store," Ben stammered.

"Him, who?" Bekka looked around Ben's shoulder.

"The guy from the theater."

"Where?" Her voice rose in pitch and volume. The look on Ben's face was freaking her out.

"Shhh!" Ben said, scowling while putting a finger to his lips. He nodded his head to the left. "He was in that aisle over there." Bekka looked in the direction he pointed.

"He saw me, but I hope he didn't recognize me."

"Let's get out of here," Bekka said, going in search of their parents. Ben kept looking back over his shoulder, the face imprinted in his memory.

In addition to the batteries, Mom had a number of items in their cart as she stood in the checkout line. Ben and Bekka stood behind her looking at key chains and jackknives, so didn't notice who was in the line next to them. When Ben looked up, he caught his breath. There he was—only ten feet from him. The man had wire and matches and a rope on the counter. Ben looked down quickly. He had no idea if the guy had spotted him or not, but he hurried out of the store with his parents after they paid for everything. What a relief to get back in the van.

"There he is," Ben said.

Bekka craned her neck to get a look at the man as she climbed into their van. He got into a brown pickup truck and sped away in the opposite direction. Loose stone flew, and dust formed a cloud behind the truck.

"Wow, look at him go," she said, excitedly.

"*That's a crazy driver,*" Mom stated. "It looks like he just robbed a bank or something."

Ben and Bekka's eyes popped open as they looked at each other. *Blowing up a bank with dynamite.* Could *that* be the plan?

Chapter 15

In less than five minutes, they arrived at the Soaring Eagle Hotel. The twins headed directly for the elevator, racing to see who could push the buttons first. One would push the button to open the elevator door and the other would push the button for the second floor. Fair and square—that's how they liked things.

"He's in Room 225," Mom informed the twins. "I'm sure he'll be ready when we get there."

When they got off at the second floor, a room door opened, and out walked their uncle. "Perfect timing. I was just about ready to call the police and issue a 'missing family' report," he joked. "I'm starving. How about a buffalo burger? Ruby's Restaurant has the best in town."

"Not me," Bekka said, crossing her arms over her chest. "I don't like buffalo burgers."

"Have you ever tried one?" her uncle asked.

"No, but I know I wouldn't like it."

"How about you, Ben? Want to try one?"

"Maybe," Ben answered. "But can I get chicken fingers, too, in case I don't like it?"

"Sure, why not? Ruby's is just down the street, so we can walk," he said as they left the hotel.

"Is Keystone a wild west town?" Bekka asked her uncle, looking at stores that must be over a hundred years old. There was even a stagecoach sitting on display in a yard.

"Yes, you could say it is. This land belonged first to the Sioux Indians, but gold was discovered in 1876, and then came the white men—all of them hoping to get rich quick. The Keystone Mine opened, and the town was named after it. There were lots of wild cowboys and rough living. The railroad finally made it here in 1920, so when they began work on Mt. Rushmore a few years later, trains brought food, dynamite, and tools. Actually, many of those 400 men who worked on Mt. Rushmore were miners who needed work because nearly all the gold had been taken out of the mines. Today more than three million people visit this area each year and we try hard to keep it looking old-fashioned. There's a shop where you can dress up in long dresses and old suits and have your picture taken. It's kind of fun. Lots of families do it to see what they might have looked like, had they lived a hundred years ago."

"I want to buy something special with my birthday money," Bekka said, looking at a street full of shops. Each store's sign advertised something different—cowboy boots, Indian jewelry, postcards, T-shirts, and Black Hills gold jewelry.

"Sounds good to me," Mom answered. "We'll do it right after we eat."

"Cool." Bekka smiled, still determined not to order a buffalo burger.

Chapter 16

"We'll have three baskets of chicken fingers, French fries, a pitcher of lemonade, and two buffalo burgers—one cut in quarters," Uncle Paul told the waitress. He winked at Bekka. He was pretty sure she would like buffalo burgers, if she would just try one.

"So, did anything exciting happen on your way here from Michigan?" he asked the twins.

"Yeah, a dog ate my dog last night," Ben answered, trying to keep a straight face.

"What? A dog ate your dog? I didn't know you had a dog," his uncle said, surprised.

"You should explain before your uncle has a heart attack," responded Dad.

Uncle Paul was practically rolling on the floor with laughter, listening to Ben's tale of Buster coming to dinner. He could just see the huge dog standing on his hind legs, helping himself to Ben's perfect hot dog.

"I assure you, no dog will enjoy your dinner tonight," he said as the waitress arrived with their food.

"Oh, this smells good," said Dad. "My stomach has been growling for two hours."

Uncle Paul took a moment to say a prayer of thanks, then smiled as he raised his buffalo burger to his lips. "Any brave people want to join me in eating the best buffalo meat in town?"

"Sure," Ben said, reaching for one of the sections of the other burger.

Mom reached for one. "Count me in." If her brother thought it was good, then she would try it too.

Dad decided to try it as well. "Bekka, how about you?" he asked. "They smell awfully good."

"Maybe when I'm done eating my chicken fingers and fries." She hoped she would be full by then.

Fifteen minutes later, all of the food on the table had been devoured except Bekka's portion of the buffalo burger. No one had keeled over dead, so she reached for it, all eyes on her. Just then, Ben grabbed his throat and started choking. She gasped and brought her hand back. If Ben was dying, it had to be the burger!

"Ben," she screamed. His face was turning red. "Are you okay?"

"Yeah," he laughed as he took his hands away from his throat. "I was just trying to scare you out of that last bite of burger."

☆★☆

Bekka punched him in the leg. "Do NOT do that to me! You scared me."

Working up courage again to try the buffalo burger, she picked it up. "Okay, I'll try a bite and then you can have the rest, Ben." Holding her nose and closing her eyes, she sank her teeth into the bun.

☆★☆

Chapter 17

Pushing the last couple of bites of his chocolate dessert around on his plate, Ben appeared quiet. Uncle Paul noticed. "Ben, you look like something is wrong. Didn't you like the buffalo burger after all?"

"It was good," he answered, "it's just that…"

"Just what?"

"Well," Ben hesitated.

"Spit it out, boy."

"Can people blow up Mt. Rushmore?"

"Ah, that might be kind of hard to do. Why?"

Still not answering the question, Ben asked, "What else can people blow up around here?"

"Well, nothing, legally. Some people still think there is gold in the old mines, but I haven't heard of anyone trying to blow up one lately," his uncle assured him. "Do you plan to do something drastic while you are here?"

Everyone broke out laughing except Ben.

"No, but somebody else might be."

His uncle got serious at that remark.

"What makes you think that?" His uncle leaned toward him, listening carefully. If someone was up to no good, he needed to know about it and report it.

"Well, when I went back to get the binoculars in the theater, I heard two men talking about blowing up something with dynamite during the fireworks."

Dad and Uncle Paul gave each other a startled look of concern. Their eyebrows jumped halfway up their foreheads. Ben may have heard the plot to something very dangerous.

"What else did you hear?" asked his uncle.

"Nothing, they asked me if I had lost something and then I got out of there."

"Did you see them again?" asked Dad.

"Yeah, at the hardware store."

"You did?" asked Mom, sounding startled. "Do you think they were following us?" She did not want her family to be involved in a crime. Their experience at Michigan's Pictured Rocks National Lakeshore Park was enough for a lifetime. But Dad was just the opposite. Being a newspaper reporter, he was always asking who, what, when, where, how, and why. He was glad Ben and Bekka seemed to have a "nose for the news" and kept him informed of what they knew.

"Were they following us?" he asked when Ben didn't answer quickly enough. "What did they look like?"

☆★☆

"I don't think they were following us. One of the guys was buying stuff."

"Stuff? Like what?" asked Uncle Paul.

"Well," Ben thought back to what he saw on the checkout counter at the store. "Matches, wire, and some rope."

"H-m-m, wire, matches, and rope. It sounds suspicious, but then it doesn't sound suspicious. You probably have wire, matches and rope in your camper."

"Yes, we do," answered Mom. Still alarmed, she asked Ben, "Did he say anything to you at the store?"

"No, but I think he knew I saw him."

"Did you see them drive away?" asked Dad.

"Yes."

"What did their car look like?"

"It wasn't a car, it was a brown truck. And they drove out of the parking lot really fast. Remember? It was the one Mom said looked like they had robbed a bank."

"You're kidding!" his father replied. "You should have said something, Ben."

Uncle Paul looked quite concerned. "These men must know how we do the fireworks. Like I said before, the fireworks at Mt. Rushmore are set off tomorrow, July third, while the ones here at Keystone go off on the Fourth of July. Therefore, if someone mentions setting off dynamite during the fireworks, which is it, on the third of July at Mt. Rushmore or the Fourth of July here in town?"

"Wow," was all Bekka could say. What had her twin stumbled into this time?

"Do you think we should inform the police or a park ranger?" asked Mom.

"I don't know," replied Uncle Paul. "We don't have much to go on, and if we make a report, we don't have much to tell them. No one knows where they live, or who they are, or what it is they plan to dynamite."

Turning to Ben and Bekka, their father said, "I think we should just keep our eyes and ears open. If you see either man or the brown truck again, tell us. That way, we'll report it at once."

"I only know what one of them looks like," Ben said. "I looked at him in the theater and he was the one in the store. The other guy must have been in the truck."

"Okay, well, at least you could identify one of them," Uncle Paul added. "Thousands of people visit Mt. Rushmore each day, and it would be easy to miss them in a crowd. There will be a lot of people here tomorrow night as well as in Keystone on the Fourth, so if they are going to blow up something, we definitely have to stop them."

Looking at his watch, Dad jumped. "Oh, my. Look what time it is. We have to get over to the campground and get the camper settled before dark. Want to join us for some s'mores later this evening, Paul?"

"Sounds good to me," he replied. "I haven't had one since I was a Boy Scout. A quiet evening around a campfire will be the perfect ending to a busy day."

✩★✩

Chapter 18

Pulling into the Circle M Campground, the twins looked around for a pool. They didn't see one, but did see a bunch of kids playing soccer. It looked like boys against the girls. The twins played on teams with the Lansing Boys and Girls Club, so they wanted to join the fun here. As their parents set up the camper, they went over to the field to see if they could play. Before long, they were trying to outrun each other to score a point.

Bekka knew Ben's tricky moves with his feet, so she was able to steal the ball from him. She smiled all the way down the field and tried to kick a goal. Luckily for the boys' team, the goalie dove for the ball and caught it. It was getting dark, and parents were on the sidelines. One dad yelled that the next goal was the last one.

Bekka badly wanted to score the last point to break a 3-3 tie. The ball rolled off the field, so Ben went after it. He shocked everybody when he did a flip as he threw it in bounds. He had learned how to do that in gymnastics and was getting to be an expert. His teammate missed the ball, and it landed right in front of Bekka. Quickly she kicked it with all her might, sending it sailing through the air over the head of the boys' goalie, right into the net. Her teammates ran over to her so fast, they almost knocked her down.

"We beat the boys! We beat the boys!" they squealed, jumping up and down. The boys were in shock.

How could they have lost to the girls?

"This calls for a celebration," Dad said, patting Bekka on the back. "The winners are invited to our campfire for s'mores."

"Yay!" the girls cheered. Bekka pointed out their campsite to her teammates.

Taking pity on Ben, who would be outnumbered, Dad invited the boys to come too. They high-fived Ben, who showed them where the campfire was.

As their new friends ran to get their own skewers, the Coopers spread the fixings for s'mores on the picnic table. Mom opened the graham crackers, Bekka unwrapped candy bars, and Ben ripped open the bag of marshmallows. He popped one in his mouth. They tasted good, roasted over a fire or straight out of the bag! Dad built a much bigger fire since it would be needed. The sun was setting and darkness fell, making the fire that much more fun. Sparks were rising way up in the air. The warmth coming from the fire felt good, as the night air up in the mountains was getting chilly.

Ben and Bekka and the others pushed marshmallows on the long-handled skewers, cooking them over the flames until they were golden brown. They smelled so good, some kids didn't wait to put them between two graham crackers with the candy bar.

They ate them right off the stick. Everybody wanted more than one s'more.

Bekka stopped roasting marshmallows to take pictures of the girls with sticky white goo around their lips. Ben couldn't help but notice how often they giggled.

Not much was left on the table when Uncle Paul arrived at ten o'clock. He quickly grabbed a skewer and put his marshmallows on it. It reminded him of when he and his sister went camping as kids and challenged each other to a marshmallow-eating contest. He always won, but he let her think she might beat him someday.

Parents came for their sons and daughters, and soon only the Coopers and Uncle Paul sat around the fire. No one spoke as the sounds of crickets got louder. The night got darker making the sky shine brighter with the summer star constellations. Uncle Paul showed Ben and Bekka how to find the North Star if they could see the handle of the Big Dipper. Then he showed them how to find the Little Dipper. Away from the lights of a city, stars could be seen more clearly.

Just then, a howl broke the quiet of the evening. Ben and Bekka jumped, wondering what it might be.

Chapter 19

"What's that?" Mom asked, remembering what she had said about not wanting to see a coyote at their campsite.

"Out here in the Black Hills, you might encounter coyotes howling at the moon or a mountain lion on the prowl," Uncle Paul explained. "They don't usually bother anyone, but it's best to stay close to your camper at night. They do leave campfires alone. There might be bears, too, so keep your food put away and don't leave any trash out. They have a very good sense of smell and want to eat what you eat."

"There are bears out here?" Bekka asked, a shiver creeping up her spine. She'd seen TV shows where bears went through trash cans when they smelled food.

"Yes, but I'm sure with all the noise here in the campground, none will come around," Uncle Paul answered. Bekka was glad they were staying in a camper and not in a tent. Her father assured her their leftovers were in the cooler in the van, which made her feel a little bit better.

"Let's change the subject," she said. "Uncle Paul, do people still find gold here?"

"I've been a geologist for a long time, looking for gold and other gems in these hills. But sad to say, there doesn't seem to be much around anymore. It used to be when miners started digging, if they found a pink stone called rose quartz, it meant gold was not far below the surface. Once in awhile some rose quartz is spotted, and people start digging. People still want to get rich quick. Mining was hard work, and many people who came out during the gold rush days went back home broke. Today, we're digging for dinosaur bones. To everyone's surprise, there were lots of dinosaurs out here in the West. We found the famous one named Sue, who is now in a museum. We'd like to add more if we can find them. Not too far from here, in a town called Hot Springs, is a large collection of woolly mammoth bones. Someday, I'd like you two to go on a dig with me."

"Co-ol," Ben exclaimed. He had visions of himself standing on a huge pile with a shovel in hand. Just then, his uncle burst his bubble.

"Funny thing, you don't dig with a shovel for bones. You use a spoon and a little paintbrush, so you don't ruin or break anything from long ago. But you just might discover something big and become famous."

"Are you famous?" asked Ben.

"Well, I'm known out here in South Dakota, but not many other places. I was invited to be the Grand Marshal of the Fourth of July parade in Keystone because of my work preserving the forests around Mt. Rushmore. The Black Hills spruce is the state tree, and I plant hundreds of them—as well as Ponderosa pine trees—each year. I'm kind of like the Johnny Appleseed of South Dakota: he planted apple seeds; I plant evergreens."

"Sweet," Bekka replied. Uncle Paul was becoming her hero.

As he stood up to leave, he said, "I suggest you return to Mt. Rushmore in the morning and then go to Keystone tomorrow afternoon before going back to see the fireworks. Touring a mine is fun, and panning for gold just might turn out to be a get-rich-quick adventure. If you find a nugget, call me. You'll be millionaires!"

Ben jumped at that one. "I'm there!" Visions of more video games danced in his head—again.

"One last thing before I go," Uncle Paul said, looking at Ben and Bekka. "I have a mystery question that comes with a reward: Mt. Rushmore didn't use to look like it does now. Whose face is in a different place? Ten dollars goes to the one who comes up with the answer."

"What?" asked Bekka. "Faces in different places?" In all her FYI reading, she hadn't seen anything about that. She would be certain to ask a ranger about it in the morning. She could buy a sweet souvenir with ten bucks.

Chapter 20

Bekka searched her travel book for the answer to her uncle's riddle while her father drove into the Black Hills the next morning. Ben watched for another herd of buffalo, but all he saw were turkey vultures circling in the sky. They went into a narrow tunnel through a mountain and as they exited, Mt. Rushmore was once again in sight.

Ranger Phil took them on a different hike around the Presidential Trail. A squirrel dashed in front of their group with a pine cone in its mouth, while another one ran after it trying to steal the pine cone. Since the attention was on the squirrels, the ranger stopped talking about Mt. Rushmore and explained how pine trees drop the cones, and then squirrels, birds, and rodents use them for food and nesting materials. He said it was another good reason to protect the environment, so animals and birds could survive. Right then Ben and Bekka weren't so interested in protecting the environment as they were in learning the answer to the mystery question, but with so many people around, they felt funny raising their hands. They hoped the ranger would mention which faces were in different places, but he didn't. As they stood directly under the presidents, they leaned their heads backward to see whether stone had been dynamited off somewhere else. Not a clue.

☆★☆

The ranger ended the tour by saying that when it rains, the water streaks the stone on Lincoln's face so it appears he is crying. Bekka wished it would rain so she could see it; Ben didn't.

All the while they walked with the ranger, Ben kept an eye out for the mystery man lurking around Mt. Rushmore. If they were going to blow something up during the fireworks, they might want to check things out one more time. Bekka wasn't as concerned about that as she was about the ten dollar reward for *faces in different places*. She put fifty cents in a big ViewMaster to look at each face up close and personal. Everything looked normal to her.

Just then, Dad came up behind them. "How about if we go back and eat lunch in Keystone before heading to Thunder Mountain Gold Mine?"

"Food!" Ben exclaimed. "I'm with ya!" He put the mystery man right out of his mind.

"Can we still pan for gold?" Bekka asked.

"Sure. Maybe one of us will strike it rich," Dad said, winking.

As they drove to Keystone on a different road, they passed an old mine with boards crossing each other in the shape of an X with a sign stating, "Keep Out!"

"Hey, look," Ben said pointing to it. "Do you think it's an old gold mine?"

"Very possibly," Dad remarked. "That's what the gold mines were like. People dug into the hills and kept going until they found gold. When the gold ran out, miners boarded up the entrance and went on to a new place. That's the history of the Black Hills."

"Sweet," Ben said, his mind imagining what life must have been like for miners.

Keystone was full of tourists and it seemed everyone wanted to eat lunch at the same time they did. The Coopers had to wait to be seated, so while Dad stood in line, Mom took Ben and Bekka to the store next door to see what Black Hills gold jewelry looked like. A video describing how it was made played continuously by the jewelry showcase.

"Can we go look at the cowboy boots?" Ben asked, tired of looking at fancy rings and things.

"I told Bekka she could pick out a necklace. You can go to the store next door, but stay there—don't leave," Mom said, firmly.

"I will, I mean I won't, I mean… I will stay in the store, I won't leave," Ben said, not sure if he was confused, but sounding kind of funny.

"Now this is a guy's store," Ben told Bekka when she and their mother finally came into the store. He had changed his mind about getting a pair of cowboy boots. "See that rattlesnake's head in a glass paperweight? That's what I'm getting for a souvenir."

"Gross," Bekka squealed. "Look at those fangs and creepy-looking eyes. Don't bring it near me."

☆★☆

Ben picked it up and put it near her face. Bekka ducked out of the way and squealed.

Mom's cell phone rang just then. It was Dad informing them they were next in line to be seated. Ben all but dashed out the door to get to the restaurant. He was going to order another buffalo burger and fries. Bekka was not.

☆★☆

Chapter 21

By two o'clock, they were done eating and were walking up to Thunder Mountain Gold Mine. Others joined their group as they put on yellow hard-hats for protection during the tour. Ben and Bekka listened attentively as the tour guide took them underground, telling stories of blasting out the mine and of the little donkeys that pulled out cartloads of gold ore. Ben looked closely at the others in their tour group to see if the mystery man might be getting information on blasting in a mine. So many ideas flew through his brain. When were they going to strike? Tonight or tomorrow on the Fourth of July?

At the end of the tour, Ben and Bekka looked forward to panning for gold. Ben was convinced he would find a nugget, making him a millionaire.

"Ben, don't get your hopes up too high," Mom cautioned.

They were given a pan with water and a scoop full of dirt. They swirled it around and around until the water drained off, and most of the dirt with it. Each one collected little specks of gold in the bottom of their pan to put in a small bottle. Ben went away disappointed he wouldn't be buying any new video games after all. Bekka knew her bottle would make a great "show-and-tell" in school.

"Before we go to the fireworks at Mt. Rushmore, we'll go back to the campground for a swim and dinner," said Dad, backing out of their parking space. "Mom has a really cool idea for dinner. More campfire cooking."

"Mmm," Bekka said. "What is it?" She enjoyed cooking and remembered the foil-pocket dinners they had made when they went to Pictured Rocks.

"Dinner in a coffee can."

"Seriously?" asked Ben. "Is it going to taste weird?"

☆★☆

"No, it's not going to taste weird. Marcia Pletz gave me the recipe. She said their family tried it last year and liked it. You can each make your own and put in what you like."

Dad looked at the kids in the rearview mirror and asked, "Should I stop and get some buffalo burgers?"

"No!" Bekka called from the backseat.

★★★
Chapter 22

Pulling out four empty coffee cans from a cupboard in the camper, Mom read the ingredients needed for "pork chop dinner in a can." Ben grabbed a bag of baby carrots from the cooler, Bekka cut up four potatoes, while Dad chopped an onion, crying just a little.

Ben teased him. "Don't cry, Dad, our dinner will taste okay."

Dad gave him a friendly poke and wiped his eyes once more. "What is it about chopping onions that makes people cry?"

Mom put a little oil in each can and added a pork chop. She took them outside and put them on the hot coals in the campfire Dad and Ben had built together. This one was just the right size for doing dinner in a can. They weren't taking any chances of setting fire to the Circle M Campground. Mom stayed right by the cans, making sure the pork chops didn't burn. When the meat looked like it was ready, she called to her family, who brought out the rest of the food. They put in as many carrots and potatoes as they wanted. Bekka and Ben agreed to put in just a little onion and topped it with some butter. Mom covered the cans with foil and set them back on the coals at the edge of the fire.

Ben and Bekka were amazed they could cook their dinner this way. Mom stirred the vegetables to make sure they cooked enough, and soon their dinner was ready to eat.

"It smells so good," Bekka said. "Can we do this at home on our grill?"

"I think we should try it," Dad said, lifting the cans carefully. The smell made Ben almost melt. He was glad Buster wasn't around to get at this food. He wondered if Caleb and Buster were still at the Twisted Creek Campground in Nebraska or if they were somewhere else. He wished he could see them again.

No one talked much as they ate their dinner. It didn't taste weird and there were no leftovers. Mom saved the cans in case they wanted to make the meal again.

"We'll leave in a few minutes to go back up to Mt. Rushmore for the fireworks," Dad said. "The ranger said they're spectacular, and we'll want to get good seats. They shine a spotlight on the faces of the presidents, and the colored glow of the fireworks is supposed to be awesome."

"I can't wait," Bekka said excitedly. They went to fireworks each year on the Fourth of July, but this sounded like it was going to be big.

Ben's thoughts went in a different direction. "Do you think those men will blow up Mt. Rushmore tonight?"

Dad and Mom looked at each other.

Dad admitted, "Uncle Paul told the rangers what you heard, but we didn't have anything more to report. They plan to have extra security people patrolling the park. Remember Ben, if you see that man again, you must tell a ranger immediately, so they can keep an eye on him."

"I will," he promised.

"Okay, let's go. Ben, make sure you look good in case you have to talk to the ranger and Bekka, you have your camera ready for any important pictures."

They each grabbed their Junior Ranger books since they had done all the projects. They planned to have their books stamped and buy a patch. It would be cool to have a collection of patches from all the National Parks they visited.

On the way to Mt. Rushmore Ben was a bit on edge. *Was he going to foil a diabolical plot and help catch two criminals in the act of blowing something up? Or was he making everyone worry for nothing?*

"Hey, Uncle Paul never told us why he needed us here at Mt. Rushmore," Bekka declared as they pulled into the parking lot.

"You're right," said Dad.

"We'll just have to wait and see," Mom said, grabbing a backpack full of snacks and drinks to eat while they watched the fireworks.

Hundreds of other people had the same idea they did, so the Coopers rode the crowded elevator to the top level and went to the outdoor amphitheater. It was getting dark, so they stayed close together. Ben walked along, minding his own business, deep in thought. Suddenly he felt a large hand grab his shoulder.

✩✭✩

Chapter 23

Just about jumping out of his skin, Ben jerked around, certain it was the man from the theater coming after him. He was ready to throw a punch.

"Wow, are you jumpy." Uncle Paul started to laugh.

"You scared me," Ben said, trying to calm down. "Where did you come from?"

"I've been waiting for you to show up." The rest of his family heard them talking and came back over to him. Ben took a good look at his uncle, surprised to see him dressed in a business suit. Noticing her uncle's clothes, Bekka asked him about it.

"Well, that's why I wanted you here at Mt. Rushmore," he began to explain. "I'm being honored tonight at the flag ceremony for all the trees I've planted this year. Each night, one scout is invited to lower and fold the flag from the flagpole out by Mt. Rushmore, and I asked if you, Ben, could be the scout to do it on my special night."

"Wow," Ben said. "Can I really do it? I don't have my uniform with me."

"Oh, yes, you do," Mom said, opening the backpack. A big smile came over her face as she pulled Ben's uniform out carefully, not wanting to wrinkle it.

"You knew about this all the time?" Bekka asked, confronting her mother. "You knew why Uncle Paul wanted us here?"

"Yes," she confessed. "Uncle Paul called asking if we could come so Ben could share this special time with him, but I had to promise not to spoil the surprise. And Bekka, you are the official photographer for the night. One of the pictures you take will be in the *Lansing State Journal* since this is something that only Boy Scouts can do."

"*Really? Really?*" Bekka asked. "One of my pictures is going to be in the newspaper?"

"Not just one newspaper, but two—the one here at Keystone and yours in Lansing," Uncle Paul informed her. Turning to Ben he said, "So, young man, you have ten minutes to get into your uniform and be out by the flagpole prepared to fold the flag."

"Wow! Can I keep the flag?" asked Ben.

"No, it goes back to the ranger who will help fold it with you," Uncle Paul replied.

Dad looked at his watch and turned to Ben, "Let's get you ready. Mom and Bekka, go get the best seats in the house."

As she sat waiting, Bekka noticed there were lots of rangers wearing hats and police with batons in their hands walking around watching people. She was glad they were taking Ben's information seriously, but she really hoped nothing would happen. A minute later, the announcer said Ben's name and he walked out to the flagpole. He and Uncle Paul were in the spotlight.

Ben was a bundle of nerves lowering the flag and getting all thirteen folds smooth. The audience was totally silent, watching his every move. His mind was freaking out—*don't drop it, you'll die of embarrassment, keep folding, you know how to do it, forget twenty thousand people are watching you.* He was excited to be folding the flag, but he sure would be glad when it was done.

Bekka got a picture of him in almost every move. He handed it to the ranger, took a step back and breathed a big sigh of relief. As the announcer talked about the hundreds of new trees Uncle Paul had planted, Ben looked up at the crowd, searching for a certain face. He wished he had his binoculars to get a closer look, but that would have looked a little too suspicious. People began to cheer as Uncle Paul received a plaque in the shape of a pine tree with his name inscribed on it. He deserved it. Bekka took his picture, too. She couldn't wait to see it in the newspaper.

People watched as Ben and Uncle Paul walked to where the family was seated. Ben wondered if the men from the theater were in the crowd watching him or were they somewhere behind the scene ready to strike?

"And now, ladies and gentlemen," the announcer said into the microphone, "What you've been waiting for—the grand display of fireworks over Mt. Rushmore."

As the lights started to dim, the Coopers noticed even more police and security guards with dogs on leashes had appeared.

"Bekka, look," Ben whispered to her as he pointed toward the small groups of police.

"Do you think they're here because they think someone might blow up Mt. Rushmore?" she asked.

"I think so."

Just then, the first boom sounded in the night sky. Red, white and blue fireworks cast a glow on the faces of the four presidents. It was spectacular, just as the ranger had said it would be. For the next twenty minutes, everyone "ooh-ed," "aah-ed," and clapped with each brilliant display. They were the biggest, the brightest, and the loudest fireworks any of them had ever seen or heard. Ben and Bekka watched them in the sky, but kept an eye on the security guards as they wandered in and out of the crowd.

To the relief of those who knew about the situation, there was no explosion at Mt. Rushmore. As people went to their cars, Uncle Paul stopped to talk to the ranger at the information desk with a lowered voice. Ben and Bekka kept looking for the man in case he might be hanging around. Guards with bomb-sniffing dogs walked down the hallway to a security room. They would go back out later to take another sniff around Mt. Rushmore. Perhaps the dynamite hadn't gone off yet, and it would after midnight when everyone had gone home.

As they traveled back to their campsite, the Coopers talked about the events of the night. Ben was still amazed that he was chosen to lower the flag, and Dad told Bekka they would have her pictures printed tomorrow, to see which one would be chosen to use in the newspaper. Little did they know how important Bekka's camera would become.

Chapter 24

The day dawned like a perfect Fourth of July should—with a blue sky and sunshine. No one wanted rain on the parade. Uncle Paul, as the Grand Marshal, was to ride in a convertible car with the top down, waving to the crowd. Ben and Bekka could hardly wait for it to start at one o'clock, so they pestered their parents to go into Keystone early so they could see everything that was going on. Getting into the spirit of the day, their parents finally agreed.

As they neared Keystone, they could see clowns with balloons and people with ice cream carts getting ready for a crowd. Old cars and fire trucks lined up in a parking lot. The smell of hot dogs and popcorn filled the air. Ben and Bekka begged for something to eat.

As Dad paid for their food, police cars raced out of town heading for Mt. Rushmore. They were followed by a fire truck. Meeting up with Uncle Paul at his hotel, he gave them the latest news as he closed his cell phone.

"Ben, you were right. There was an explosion."

"Where?" exclaimed Ben and Bekka together.

"In an abandoned mine on a road behind Mt. Rushmore. Sure enough, they must have been plotting it when you went into the theater for your binoculars. People going home after the fireworks last night saw smoke coming out of the mine and came here to Keystone to report it. By the time the police got there, the bad guys were gone."

"Do they know who did it yet?" asked Mom.

"No."

"Wow," Bekka said.

"You'll have to keep your eyes open around town in case the two guys you saw show up," Dad said to Ben.

"Bekka, how about you and I go to the camera shop over there and have your pictures printed out?" Mom said. "We can show Uncle Paul the ones you took of him and Ben last night at Mt. Rushmore."

"We guys will wait out here watching people coming for the parade," Dad said, as three kids ran by with flags in their hands.

In a few minutes, Bekka had the printed pictures in hand. Everyone looked at them as they stood on the sidewalk.

"There he is!" Ben yelled, as he looked at one picture. "There he is."

"Who is?" asked Uncle Paul, looking over Ben's shoulder at the picture. It was one of the photos he had taken of Ben and Bekka at Mt. Rushmore, when a man had walked behind them.

"The man I saw in the theater and the store!" Ben exclaimed.

☆★☆

"Let me see it closer," Dad said. "We need to turn this in to the police. The only trouble is, we don't have proof they are the ones who blew up the mine."

"At least if the police see his face, they can keep an eye out for him," Uncle Paul said. "The station is right over there. Let's go."

As they crossed the street, out of the police station came a boy and his dog.

"Caleb! Buster!" yelled Bekka. Ben jerked his head up and almost tripped on the sidewalk.

✩★✩

Chapter 25

"What are you doing here?" Ben asked. Buster was dragging Caleb toward them. "How'd you get here?"

"I live here in Keystone," Caleb explained. "We were on vacation at Twisted Creek 'til last night when my dad got a call to bring Buster back. He's a dynamite-sniffing dog and he had to go into the mine this morning to see if there is any more dynamite there after last night's explosion. He didn't find any, so my dad brought him back into town and said I could take him for a walk."

"We think we know who did it," Ben said.

"You do?" Caleb asked, his eyes getting as big as saucers.

Ben began the story. "I heard two guys talking at the Visitor Center about blasting dynamite during the fireworks, but I only got a good look at one of them. Later, my uncle accidentally got a picture of his face. Look," Ben said, showing Caleb the photograph. "We're taking it to the police right now."

"Wow," was all Caleb could say. It was so cool that his new friends could help solve this crime!

Uncle Paul took the picture from Ben. "How about you and Bekka stay out here with Caleb and Buster while we three adults go talk to the police? Here's five dollars to get an ice cream. The parade doesn't start for another hour. Walk around and have fun. We'll meet you in front of the hardware store down there where my Grand Marshal's car is parked."

"OK," said Ben, as the three of them headed toward the other end of town.

People were already setting up lawn chairs on the sidewalks to get a good view of the parade. Side streets were blocked off to prevent cars from parking near the parade route. Bands practiced in the park, adding to the excitement. A train whistle blew on the far end of the street, sending a big puff of black smoke into the air.

"There's an old train sitting down there," Bekka said, not believing she was seeing one on the track not far from them.

"Yeah, it's, like, over a hundred years old," Caleb said. "And it doesn't go far, just up over the mountain to Hill City and then it comes back here. You should ride it—it's sweet. The whistle means it's gonna leave."

Ben was about to say something when his mouth fell open.

⭐⭐⭐

Chapter 26

"There he is," Ben exclaimed.

"Who?" asked Bekka.

"Him!" Ben exclaimed, pointing toward the track. Standing in line to board the train was the man from the theater.

"Where?" asked Bekka. Caleb didn't know who he was looking for, so he looked where Ben pointed.

"He's getting on the train!" Ben exclaimed, even louder.

Ben's voice was getting so loud people turned and looked at him. Ben's and the man's eyes locked as they recognized each other. The man pulled his cowboy hat down further over his eyes, moved faster toward the steps, and climbed aboard. He knew he had been spotted.

"We gotta tell the police! We gotta find Dad and Mom!" Bekka said, heading back toward the police station on a dead run. Caleb, Buster, and Ben were hot on her heels, almost tripping on the legs of lawn chairs in their way. Buster tried to stop at a fire hydrant for a sniff, but Caleb pulled him along as he ran.

Just as they reached the police station, the door opened and out walked their parents and Uncle Paul.

"Dad! Mom! We saw the man!" Ben yelled. "We really did!"

✩✩✩

"Where?" asked Dad, looking up the street where the kids had come from.

"He got on the old train down there," Bekka said, pointing. A puff of smoke appeared and the whistle blew again, signaling the train's departure from the station.

"What can we do?" asked Mom, looking toward Uncle Paul.

"It's the old 1881 train that goes up to Hill City. It doesn't stop between here and there, so he'll be getting off there. I'll go back in to tell the police, but you'll have to help identify him, Ben. I have to stay here for the parade, but you all should go in your van and be in Hill City when the train arrives. You've got a half-hour's drive, so you'd better get going."

"Can Caleb go with us?" Ben asked. "Maybe he and Buster can help us capture him."

"I can ask my mom," Caleb said quickly, before anyone could refuse. "I live right down that street. See that green house?"

☆☆☆

Thinking a service dog might help, Dad agreed. "I'll suggest they send Caleb's dad up in a patrol car in case Buster is needed. Okay, you kids go with Mom to ask Caleb's mother while I get the van," Dad said, looking at his watch. "I'll be there in less than five minutes." With that, he was off and running toward the parking lot.

Mom herded the three kids and dog safely across the street toward Caleb's house. His mother was surprised to see all of them standing at the door.

"Mom, this is Ben and Bekka," Caleb said, looking up at her. "Remember I told you about Buster eating somebody's hot dog at the campground the other day? Well, that was Ben's." His mother smiled as she remembered the story. "They came here to Mt. Rushmore and they think they know who blew up the mine, and the man got on the train, and they are going to go find him in Hill City, and they want to know if Buster and I can go with them. Can I go, please? Their Uncle Paul is going to have Dad ride up in a patrol car in case Buster is needed."

The words tumbled out so fast his mother could hardly keep up with his train of thought. Looking at Mrs. Cooper, she asked, "Is this true?"

"Yes," Mrs. Cooper said. "I'm Amy Cooper. When we were at Mt. Rushmore two days ago, Ben overheard two men planning to set off dynamite during the fireworks. My brother Paul, who is the Grand Marshal of the parade, accidentally got one of the men in a picture with the twins, and we just discovered it when we had them printed out. Paul is at the police station right now with the picture to identify him. We feel we can help the police in Hill City spot him when he gets off the train. We won't be long. We plan to be back in time for the parade."

"Well, okay. Maybe Buster can help sniff out something. We don't have this kind of excitement around here much," remarked Caleb's mother. "Keystone is a quiet little town and we like to keep it that way."

Just then, a horn blew behind them. Dad drove the van into the driveway and jerked to a stop. Everyone ran to open a door and climb in. Ben and Caleb got into the back seats while Bekka got in the middle row. Buster took one look at the empty spot next to her, jumped onto it, and licked her face.

"Buster!" she said, pushing him away. "Yuck!" The boys laughed at her disgust.

"The main street is blocked off, so I had to find a shortcut to get here," Dad said to Caleb. "Can you tell me the fastest way to the road to Hill City?"

"I think so. Just go down our street and go left at that light down there. Then you have to take the road up the hill," Caleb said, moving his arm left and right and up toward the ceiling of the van.

Dad drove as fast as he safely could, and soon they were going up, up, and still up, over the mountain toward Hill City. They saw puffs of smoke ahead of them. Everyone hoped they could beat the train.

"Oh, no," Dad exclaimed. "Something's in the road ahead. Cars are stopping."

Sure enough, two buffalo were crossing the road and people were stopping to take pictures.

"Pass them, Dad," Ben shouted from his seat in the back, as they slowed down to a crawl.

"I can't see over the hill," Dad said leaning left to get a better view for cars coming toward them.

"We have to beat the train," Bekka said urgently.

Dad cautiously passed the stopped cars and then sped up again. It was going to be close if they were to beat the train to the top. Ben, Bekka, and Caleb strained their necks looking for the caboose as they turned a corner. Black smoke drifted in their direction.

☆★☆

Chapter 27

"Oh, no, we didn't make it," Mom said. "People are getting off the train." People were crowding around the train to go back down to Keystone, making it hard to tell who was coming or going.

The Coopers, Caleb, and Buster climbed out of the van as fast as they could, while trying hard to see those getting off the train. The man was nowhere in sight.

"We missed him," Ben moaned as the conductor climbed down the steps, allowing new passengers to get on.

"Let's walk toward downtown and see if we can spot him," Dad said, hoping Ben could see him on the sidewalk or in a store. They were only two blocks from the main street of Hill City.

"Wow, what's going on here?" asked Mom, seeing a huge crowd of people on each side of the street.

"People dress up in old fashioned clothes and do a Wild West shoot-out in the street," Caleb informed her. "They have good guys and bad guys, and ask visitors if they want to do it with them."

"How will we ever be able to find the man?" Bekka asked. "Everybody looks like a cowboy."

"Buster!" Caleb said excitedly. "He can sniff dynamite on a person's hands and clothes. If we walk around everybody, he'll find him."

Dad pulled everyone together in a quick huddle. "Until Caleb's dad and the policeman from Keystone get here, I'm going to go find a policeman. Stay together as a group. If you spot him, have Buster hold on to him until I get back."

Giving Dad some time to find the police station, Mom kept everyone together as they watched the Wild West drama in the street. After a few minutes, they began walking along the sidewalk, looking for anyone with a cowboy hat pulled down over his eyes. Unfortunately, hundreds of cowboys had their hats pulled down. The sun was directly overhead, making it bright for everyone's eyes. If they were going to catch the man, it would have to be with Buster's help.

Caleb let Buster walk as close to people as he could without bumping into them, but Buster didn't smell dynamite on anyone. They got to the end of the street and crossed over to the other side. Mom saw a jewelry store that looked interesting and was about to go inside when Buster started to growl. Caleb recognized the sound instantly and looked at the person who Buster was focused on. Leaning against the outside wall of the store with his foot pulled up against it was a man with his hat pulled down. No one would suspect him of a crime. He looked like a tourist trying to watch the street show.

The announcer asked for visitors to come and be a part of the show. The man quickly volunteered and walked into the street.

Caleb didn't know if he should let Buster take him down or not. Ben didn't get excited at seeing the man, so Caleb asked him, "Is that the man you saw?"

"No, why?"

"Buster was growling, and I almost let him attack, but you didn't recognize him, so I didn't," Caleb said.

"That's not him."

The door opened behind them and a person stepped out. Buster growled again, lifting his head toward the man's pant leg. The growl got louder. Ben looked up and gasped. It was the face of the man from Mt. Rushmore!

Chapter 28

Caleb heard Ben gasp and knew it was the man from the theater. Caleb had to hold tightly to Buster as he growled and pulled on his leash. The man started to walk away quickly, and Buster pulled harder on his leash, breaking free. Sensing the dog was coming for him, the man started running.

"Get 'em, Buster," Caleb yelled as Ben, Bekka, and Mom took off running after the man too. Grabbing the man's leg, Buster held on until the man fell to the ground.

☆★☆

"Stay," commanded Caleb as they reached Buster.

"Call your dog off," yelled the man, "or you'll be sorry." He was yanking and pulling, trying to get free, but Buster had a tight grip on his jeans.

"No way, mister," Caleb responded. "Ben, do you see your dad anywhere?"

They were all looking up and down the street for Dad or a policeman. A crowd was starting to form around them.

"There he is!" Mom exclaimed as she spotted him. He was still a block away.

"Dad! Dad!" Ben and Bekka both yelled together, cupping their hands around their mouths.

Their father had two policemen walking beside him, one of them using a walkie talkie. Clearing away the spectators, they approached Caleb and Buster who still had the man pinned to the ground.

"Good boy," the policeman said, slowly approaching Buster. Turning toward Caleb, he said, "You can release him now."

Caleb gave a pull on Buster's leash, signaling he could let go of the man's pant leg. Getting up, the man tried to get away, but both policemen grabbed him.

"Keep that dog away from me," the man exclaimed to the policemen. He was afraid of Buster, so he took a step backward. "Why are you doing this to me?"

"We have reason to believe you blew up the old Baxter Mine by Mt. Rushmore last night," answered one of the policemen.

"You don't have proof I was even near Mt. Rushmore or a mine," retorted the man.

"Sure we do, thanks to these kids and their dog."

"What proof?" asked the startled man.

"We have a picture of you taken at Mt. Rushmore just the other day, and Buster here is a dynamite-sniffing dog," the other policeman said, stroking Buster's head. "He's never wrong when he sniffs dynamite on someone's clothes. He's top dog around here. You just might call him 'Dy-no-mite'!"

A large crowd had gathered, watching them rather than the street show. Suddenly Buster began his low growling again.

☆★☆

Chapter 29

Caleb took the leash and let Buster take a few steps down the street. A man who had been watching them, was moving quickly toward a brown truck parked next to the curb. Buster took off running after him, grabbed his leg, and knocked him down.

"Call off your dog," the man yelled.

"No!" Caleb yelled back to him. One of the policemen ran over to them. Ben and Bekka were close behind.

"Get your dog off me, or I'll sue!" the man shouted.

"We just want to ask you some questions," the policeman said. "Where are you going in such a hurry?"

"Nowhere. I was just going to get in my truck when this dog attacked me."

Ben and Bekka looked up at the man's truck and recognized it immediately. It was the same one that had flown out of the parking lot at the hardware store in Keystone.

"He's that man's partner," Ben exclaimed, pointing to the other guy Buster had chased. "We saw them in this truck the day they were at Mt. Rushmore."

"Yeah," Bekka added.

"Call your dog off!" the man demanded again.

"Not until I give you a pair of Hill City bracelets," replied the policeman as he handcuffed the man's wrists. "He's a dynamite-sniffing dog, and we have reason to believe you and your partner blew up the old Baxter Mine last night. I think we'll let Buster have a little sniff around your truck to see if he finds traces of dynamite in it. If he does, you're busted!"

Caleb and Ben grabbed Buster's leash and headed toward the truck. Holding the man's arm, the policeman followed close behind. He opened the driver's door and let Buster sniff inside. In less than three seconds, Buster let out a growl, tipping off the policeman that he had smelled dynamite. He got on the radio connected to his shoulder to call in backup.

Throughout the drama, Bekka kept her camera busy, taking pictures of Buster on the ground with each of the men and Buster sniffing the truck. He was a hero! Buster had busted the men.

A police car arrived and took the men away. Word was spreading that the crooks who blew up the Baxter Mine had been caught right there in Hill City, and the mystery had been solved by three kids and a dog. People cheered as the family walked back to the van.

Dad's cell phone rang. After answering it, a startled look came across his face. "We'll be there as soon as we can," he said. Shutting his phone, he took off for Keystone as soon as everyone was buckled in.

☆★☆

Chapter 30

Dad didn't say much as they drove back down the hills toward Keystone. Mom looked straight ahead. Ben and Bekka couldn't get any information out of them, so they quit asking. Caleb sat looking out the window, thinking about what had just happened with Buster and those men. Buster sat happily on the seat next to Bekka as if nothing had happened.

"All buffalo had better stay out of our way," Dad said seriously and drove a little faster.

Arriving in Keystone, Ben and Bekka expected the parade to be half over, but thousands of people still sat waiting in lawn chairs and on the curb.

"I wonder what's going on," Caleb said as he looked around. "The parade never waits for anything."

Dad parked the car and instructed everyone to get out and head for the hardware store.

"Why?" asked Ben.

"You'll see," Mom said, still looking kind of serious.

As they got closer, they saw Uncle Paul's Grand Marshal's convertible car still in first position, ready to take off. Bands and fire trucks were behind him. He motioned for them to come over by his car.

"What happened, Uncle Paul?" Bekka asked. "Why isn't the parade going?"

"Word spreads quickly around here," Uncle Paul explained. "When we heard what you did at Hill City, catching the guys who blew up the mine, the mayor insisted we wait for you to come back to Keystone. You kids are to ride in the Grand Marshal's car with me. Hurry and climb in. Buster, you get the front seat by the driver."

They wasted no time hopping into the backseat and climbing up on the back ledge. Buster looked out the front window, sitting as proud as a peacock.

"Let the parade begin!" yelled Uncle Paul, as his car started moving forward. Dad and Mom couldn't have been prouder of their children, Caleb, and especially Buster. They watched all three kids wave to the crowd, who cheered and clapped for them. Who would have thought a dog eating a hot dog would lead to a friendship that would lead to three kids solving a crime with a camera and a dynamite-sniffing dog?

Newspaper reporters were waiting at the end of the parade to interview Ben, Bekka, and Caleb. Cameras flashed in their faces 'til they couldn't smile any longer. Buster was proclaimed the real hero of the day.

Caleb's parents invited everyone to their house for a hot dog roast, but this time Buster was not allowed anywhere near Ben's plate. He was in his doghouse enjoying the biggest doggie treat to be found in all of Keystone.

THE END

Interesting Facts About Mount Rushmore

1. Mount Rushmore is also known as the Shrine of Democracy.

2. The four presidents carved in the mountain are George Washington, Thomas Jefferson, Theodore Roosevelt, and Abraham Lincoln.

3. 400 drillers and carvers worked on the project under the direction of Gutzon Borglum. No one died while building the monument.

4. It took 14 years to complete Mount Rushmore, from 1927 to 1941.

5. The sculpture cost $989,992.32 to build.

6. Over 1.7 billion pounds of stone were removed using dynamite, detailed drilling, and finishing processes.

7. There is a cave behind the carving called the "Hall of Records". Construction began in July of 1938. A 70-foot tunnel was blasted into the mountain. Work ended July of 1939 because of a lack of money. Mr. Borglum died in 1941 and construction ended. In 1998 the National Park service and members of the Borglum family inserted the United States Constitution, as well as other documents, and sealed the vault.

8. The carving of Thomas Jefferson was originally started on George Washington's right. However, after 18 months they realized that it was not working. Jefferson's face was dynamited off and carved on the other side. *(Answer to "Uncle Paul's" mystery question— "faces in different places".)*

Mt. Rushmore Photo Gallery

Photos used by permission from Mt. Rushmore National Monument

Follow Ben and Bekka from Lansing, Michigan to Mt. Rushmore in South Dakota.

It is 1,055 miles from Lansing, Michigan, to Mt. Rushmore in South Dakota. Can you find those two states on the map? (Hint: their abbreviations are MI & SD) Mt. Rushmore is to the left of the star in South Dakota.

Interesting facts about South Dakota:

1. The capital city is Pierre.

2. The state bird is the Ring-necked Pheasant.

3. The state flower is the Pasqueflower, also known as Prairie Crocus.

4. The state tree is the Black Hills Spruce (picea glauca).

5. It became a state on November 2, 1889 (39th or 40th— admitted the same day as North Dakota).

6. Its motto is "Under God the People Rule".

7. Its nickname is "Mt. Rushmore State" or "Coyote State".

8. The state song is "Hail, South Dakota".

9. The number of square miles: 77,121.

10. Border states: Iowa, Minnesota, Montana, Nebraska, North Dakota, and Wyoming.

Why the Flag is Folded Thirteen times

Boy Scout Script (not official)

1. In honor of the thirteen original colonies and our forefathers who founded this great nation, we salute you.

2. To the men who died in the War for Independence, we salute you.

3. To those men who fell in the War of 1812, to preserve our freedom, we salute you.

4. To the brave soldiers on both sides, The North and The South, in the Civil War, we salute you.

5. To those who shed their blood in the name of hope and freedom in The Great War, we salute you.

6. For our fathers and sons who died in the terrible battles of World War Two, Pearl Harbor, Anzio, Midway, The Bulge, Iwo Jima, Guadalcanal, Normandy, and Berlin, we salute you.

7. To the men of the First Marine Division, who, in a rear guard action at the Chosin Reservoir in Korea saved their battalion and the lives of their brother Marines, we salute you.

8. For the brave men and women of our armed forces who died on the fields of fire in Vietnam and whose names will live on forever on that hallowed wall, we salute you.

9. For our commander in chief, who leads our nation in good times, and bad, we salute you.

10. For the Boy Scouts of America and all the Scouts who have gone before us, we salute you.

11. To God, our parents and our families who we love and respect, we salute you.

12. To the men and women of our armed forces, the Arsenal of Democracy and the Hammer of Freedom, we salute you.

13. And last, to freedom, because without freedom there is no honor, without honor, we are not Americans, and on this we vow, that as long as this flag flies, we salute you.

Native American Indian Facts

1. **Where does the name Sioux (pronounced sue) come from?** *It is not a Lakota or Dakota tribal name. It comes from the Ojibway name which means "little snakes."*

2. **What is the difference between Lakota and Dakota Sioux?** *There is no difference—some Sioux alphabets have the letter L in it, some do not. They all consider themselves part of the same culture.*

3. **Where do the Sioux live?** *The first Lakota/Dakota Indians lived in what is now North and South Dakota, Wisconsin, and Minnesota. Today they also live in Iowa, Illinois, Montana, Nebraska, and parts of Canada.*

4. **What language do the Sioux people speak?** *Nearly all speak English, but about 15,000 still speak their native language.*

5. **How do Sioux Indian children live, and what did they do in the past?** *They do what most children do—go to school, play with friends, and do chores around the house. They used to have more chores which meant less time to play. They had dolls and toys to play with.*

6. **What was Sioux clothing like? Did they wear feather headdresses and face paint?** *Sioux women wore long deerskin or elkskin dresses, while men wore leggings and buckskin shirts. They made moccasins for their feet and buffalo-hide robes in bad weather. Warriors and chiefs were known for their feathered warbonnets, but didn't wear them every day. Everyone wore their hair long and in braids. They painted their faces and arms with bright colors and animal designs. Different patterns were used for warpaint and festive decoration.*

7. **How did the Sioux travel?** *The Sioux walked most places but learned to make birchbark and dugout canoes. They used dogs to pull travois—a type of dog sled to move their belongings. Europeans introduced them to horses and they became famous as riders. Today they use modern cars and trucks.*

Native Languages of the Americans—Laura Redish and Orrin Lewis
www.native-languages.org

Lakota Sioux Animal Words

Native Languages of the Americans—Laura Redish and Orrin Lewis
www.native-languages.org/lakota_animals.htm

sunka	sunkawakan	tatanka	hexaka
sunkmanitu tanka	mato	igmuwatogla	sungila
wiciteglega	pahin	mastinca	zica
zintkala	anunkasan	maga	hinhan
zuzeca	hogan	keva	tuhmunga

Camping Recipes

PORK CHOP IN A CAN

Place 2 tablespoons of oil in the bottom of a clean coffee can.

Place a pork chop in the bottom of the can.

Cook over coals on the side of a campfire.

After a few minutes, flip it over using a long handled fork.

Add a peeled carrot, cut-up potato, and a slice of onion.

Top with a tablespoon of butter.

Put aluminum foil on top of the can and put back
over the coals, cooking for 45 minutes.

Remove from heat, let it cool for a few
minutes, and flip out onto a plate.

ENJOY!

S'MORES

Place 2 marshmallows on a skewer and roast over a campfire.

When they are golden brown, remove
and put on one half of a graham cracker.

Layer one half of a flat chocolate bar on top
and add the other graham cracker.

ENJOY!

WHO, WHAT, WHEN, WHERE, AND WHY?

1. Who are the two main characters in this book?
2. Who do they meet in Nebraska?
3. Where were the Coopers traveling to?
4. What funny thing happened at the campground's picnic table?
5. Why did Uncle Paul want them to meet him there?
6. What important holiday was celebrated in the book?
7. What did Ben hear the men in the theater say to each other?
8. What didn't Bekka want to eat at the Ruby Restaurant in Keystone?
9. Where did they catch the bad guys?
10. Why was each president chosen?
11. What American Indian tribe is Caleb from?
12. What new things did you learn?

MEET THE CHARACTERS

Bekka	Ben	Caleb

Real life twins Hannah and Ethan Hopewell
and their friend Caleb Allen

Where in the USA are Ben and Bekka Going?

Using the coded alphabet, uncover the spelling of the next National Park the Coopers will visit. Below is a clue—can you guess it before you decode it?

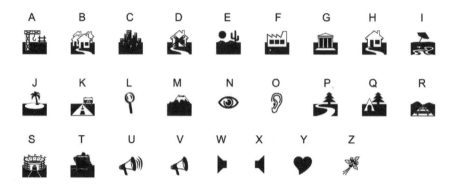

A CLUE:

Before Colonel Custer went to South Dakota,
he fought in the Civil War at this city.

THE ANSWER:

____ ____ ____ ____ ____ ____ ____ ____ ____ ____

____ ____ ____ ____ ____ ____ ____ ____ ____ ____ ____